Bird swooshed down the banister into Murphy's waiting arms. She hugged him and gave his cheek a damp kiss.

As his eyes met Phoebe's, Murphy felt a tightness in his chest. He'd seen her protectiveness with her child. But Phoebe trusted him with her daughter.

He didn't know why that mattered—but it did.

Bird gazed up at him adoringly. "I don't got a daddy, but you can be my Murphy."

He grasped her hand, and a curious tickling in his throat made him cough. "I'd be honored to be your...Murphy."

"Well, of course. Because everybody's got to have somebody. Now you belong to me." She closed her fist around his thumb. "Okay?"

"Okay," he said. The feel of her small hand clinging to his turned his heart over. And nothing could describe the rush of emotions swirling through him as Phoebe's daughter looked at him steadily with her trusting, innocent eyes....

Dear Reader,

Silhouette Romance blends classic themes and the challenges of romance in today's world into a reassuring, fulfilling novel. And this month's offerings undeniably deliver on that promise!

In *Baby, You're Mine*, part of BUNDLES OF JOY, RITA Award-winning author Lindsay Longford tells of a pregnant, penniless widow who finds sanctuary with a sought-after bachelor who'd never thought himself the marrying kind...until now. Duty and passion collide in Sally Carleen's *The Prince's Heir*, when the prince dispatched to claim his nephew falls for the heir's beautiful adoptive mother. When a single mom desperate to keep her daughter weds an ornery rancher intent on saving his spread, she discovers that *McKenna's Bartered Bride* is what she wants to be...forever. Don't miss this next delightful installment of Sandra Steffen's BACHELOR GULCH series.

Donna Clayton delivers an emotional story about the bond of sisterhood...and how a career-driven woman learns a valuable lesson about love from the man who's *Her Dream Come True*. Carla Cassidy's MUSTANG, MONTANA, Intimate Moments series crosses into Romance with a classic boss/secretary story that starts with the proposition *Wife for a Week*, but ends...well, you'll have to read it to find out! And in Pamela Ingrahm's debut Romance novel, a millionaire CEO realizes that his temporary assistant—and her adorable toddler—have him yearning to leave his *Bachelor Boss* days behind.

Enjoy this month's titles—and keep coming back to Romance, a series guaranteed to touch *every* woman's heart.

Mary-Theresa Hussey

Mary-Theresa Hussey
Senior Editor

Please address questions and book requests to:
Silhouette Reader Service
U.S.: 3010 Walden Ave., P.O. Box 1325, Buffalo, NY 14269
Canadian: P.O. Box 609, Fort Erie, Ont. L2A 5X3

BABY, YOU'RE MINE

Lindsay Longford

Silhouette ROMANCE™
Published by Silhouette Books
America's Publisher of Contemporary Romance

To my sisters-in-law Barbara Cross, Marty Cross,
Bonnie Kasowski and Lois Vangundy

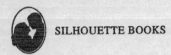 SILHOUETTE BOOKS

ISBN 0-373-19396-3

BABY, YOU'RE MINE

Copyright © 1999 by Jimmie Morel

Visit us at www.romance.net

Printed in U.S.A.

Books by Lindsay Longford

Silhouette Romance

Jake's Child #696
Pete's Dragon #854
Annie and the Wise Men #977
The Cowboy, the Baby and the
  Runaway Bride #1073
The Cowboy and the
  Princess #1115
Undercover Daddy #1168
Daddy by Decision #1204
A Kiss, a Kid and a
  Mistletoe Bride #1336
Baby, You're Mine #1396

Silhouette Intimate Moments

Cade Boudreau's Revenge #390
Sullivan's Miracle #526
Renegade's Redemption #769
No Surrender #947

Silhouette Shadows

Lover in the Shadows #29
Dark Moon #53

LINDSAY LONGFORD,

like most writers, is a reader. She even reads toothpaste labels in desperation! A former high school English teacher with an M.A. in literature, she began writing romances because she wanted to create stories that touched readers' emotions by transporting them to a world where good things happened to good people and happily-ever-after is possible with a little work.

Her first book, *Jake's Child,* was nominated for Best New Series Author, Best Silhouette Romance, and received a Special Achievement Award for Best First Series Book from *Romantic Times Magazine.* It was also a finalist for the Romance Writers of America's RITA Award for Best First Book. Her Silhouette Romance novel *Annie and the Wise Men* won the RITA for Best Traditional Romance of 1993.

Dear Reader,

Bundles. That's what babies are. Each one is a wrapped-up surprise package, a bundle of hopes and terrors.

Our failures cease to exist in their love. They love us unconditionally, and we see ourselves through their eyes. We become that all-powerful, good person who knows everything, who can solve any crisis, who fills our child's heart with joy. Their love makes us do anything, brave everything, to keep them safe. For those few moments in time we are perfect for at least one person in this world. Well, at least until they turn into those equally fascinating creatures known as teenagers!

For our children we reach out to the world and look at it differently. For me, my son became a small vessel I could fill with all the fairy tales and myths I'd loved. He gave me a chance to again read books that I'd grown too old for. And, night after night, I told him stories, always with a brown-eyed boy as the hero. Sometimes he would tap me on the shoulder as I drifted asleep and beg, "Don't stop. Keep telling the story." And, captive to his delight, I would continue.

Children teach us to view the people in our lives in a new way. My love for my husband deepened after I saw how our infant son reached in and with one powerful, baby grip grabbed and held on to my husband's heart for the rest of his life, enriching it and giving it meaning, changing him.

Reminding us of life's fragility, our babies teach us to fill each moment with love, to make every moment count. They are a gift, these babies, our bundles of incredible joy.

With affection and joy,

Lindsay Longford

Chapter One

Fanning herself with the folded *Manatee Creek News* she'd found on the stoop, Phoebe huddled in the porch swing, suitcases piled beside the front door.

Sooner or later Murphy would come home. He had to.

Because she'd just bet her last dime that he would be here. No, not her actual *last* dime. After buying the plane tickets and paying the taxi from the airport, she had fifty dollars left. Heck, by some folks' standards, she reckoned she should count herself a wealthy woman.

The swing creaked, rusty chain rubbing against wicker and metal, the sound loud in the hot afternoon silence.

Her daughter's sticky body was plastered tight against Phoebe as the little girl kicked the swing back and forth with both sneakered feet. Her small, pointed face was peony-pink from the heat.

"Nice breeze." Lightly tapping the end of Frances

Bird's button nose, Phoebe lifted a hank of sweat-damp hair away from her own neck. "Thanks, baby. Every little breath of air helps."

In the heat and humidity, Phoebe's fine, curly hair stuck to her cheek, frizzed. Her lipstick had worn off hours earlier, and the makeup she'd applied so carefully in the fresh morning air of Wisconsin had long ago melted off her face. If she could muster the energy, she supposed she ought to slather on a bright red lipstick, show Murphy a happy face. And she would, too, once she found an ounce of get-up-and-go. Giving credit where credit was due, though, she *had* gotten up and gone. But now she was here.

And here she'd stay.

Until she talked with Murphy.

The swing wobbled, tilted, as Frances Bird shifted. "I'm thirsty, Mama. I want a cool drink, and I *need* it now."

"Patience, Bird." She tugged her not-quite-a-baby to her. The warm, little-girl scent rose to Phoebe, and she rested her cheek against her daughter's sweaty forehead and inhaled.

Terrifying, the weight of all this love.

With a wiggle, Frances Bird braced her heels against the wooden porch boards and shoved, sending the swing careening to one side. "Don't have any patience left. I am *parched*," she said, all reasonableness as she stuck her face close to Phoebe's. "And I would very much like a soda pop. With ice."

At the moment, Phoebe would have settled for ice. A bucket full. She'd dump ice down the neck of her T-shirt, slick the coolness over her neck.

"Maybe there's a water spigot on the side of the

house." Standing up, Phoebe took Bird's hand. "That's the best I can do right now, dumpling."

"If it has to be, it has to be," Frances Bird said on a long sigh, straight-as-a-stick brown hair flopping into her eyes.

Watching her daughter's woebegone expression, Phoebe decided the McAllister women were into sighing altogether too much. Sighing could become a real unattractive habit if she didn't watch herself. She allowed her voice to take on an edge of tartness. "Come on, Frances Bird. Don't mope. It'll be an adventure."

"Won't be." Frances Bird stood and clumped down the stoop with Phoebe, sneakers smacking each step.

They found the spigot at the back of Murphy's house. "What a mess." Frowning, Phoebe yanked at the weeds and woody vines screening the lumpy hose lying on the sandy ground. She wrapped the hem of her T-shirt around the hot metal faucet and twisted. Sun-heated, the hose bucked and heaved in her hands, spewing brown water into her eyes and down her arms. "Whoa!"

"Yuck." Frances Bird leaped backward and wrinkled her nose at the murky brown water splashing onto her legs. "Hot!"

"Water's water, sugar-dumpling. Let it run. It'll cool in a second. And when it does," Phoebe smiled teasingly and waggled the hose at her, "you're going to be all wet, my darling girl."

"No!" Frances Bird darted behind Phoebe. "*You.* Not me." She wrestled for the hose, and Phoebe let the soft plastic uncoil into Frances Bird's hands. Soaking them, water sprayed and splashed in sparkling drops that clung to Frances Bird's hair like a rainbow halo.

"It's as cool as it's going to be." Phoebe held the hose steady while her daughter drank. "Well, dumpling, good thing you're not all dressed up. You have as much water outside you as in."

Frances Bird shook her head. Water arched, then silvered down to the ground. Looking up, she smiled. "Yes. Water," she said blissfully and jumped feet first into the mud, happy for the first time that day.

Phoebe let her play. There was no rush. They weren't going anywhere.

Squashing down her anxiety, she chased Frances Bird. Bird chased her back until they were both breathless, their bare feet covered in pale mud. "Enough, enough," Phoebe finally panted as she shook sopping strands of hair out of her eyes.

With one final spray of the hose for each of them, she turned off the spigot, leaving the hose neatly coiled underneath. When they returned to the front of the house and its empty driveway, anxiety twisted the knots in her stomach tighter.

Still no Murphy. What would they do if he didn't come home until after midnight? What if he'd gone out of town? She should have called, she knew she should have. Oh, what a fool she'd been not to call.

But she hadn't. Couldn't.

Every woman had her limits. She'd hit hers.

Hiding her apprehension, she plopped down on the step beside Frances Bird, gasping, but finally, blessedly cool.

The sun was edging the tip of the thick, mossdraped branches of the live oaks at the front of Murphy's house when she heard the rumble of an engine.

She didn't have time to catch her breath. He was just there, climbing slowly out of his cobalt-blue pickup, ambling right up to the foot of the stairs, his big, dark shadow falling over her. Murphy never moved fast. Like glaciers, he took his own sweet time.

"Hey, Murphy," she said and stayed seated. Lord knew her knees would buckle if she stood up. Water still dripped from the ends of her hair, down the back of her T-shirt. "Long time, and all that." She couldn't seem to get a good breath. She rested one palm lightly on Frances Bird's head. With her other, she gestured to the stash of cans and sawhorses in the back of his truck. "Busy?"

Strings hung from the armholes of his sleeveless, washed-to-cobwebs shirt. By the grace of God and a miracle of thread, one button clung to the placket of his shirt. Sweat-plastered to his ribs, the shirt hung open, revealing a narrow streak of hair bleached to sunshine gold. Glowing in the bright light, that tapered line drew her gaze unwillingly down the taut muscles of his chest to the waistband of paint-kaleidoscoped jeans, jeans so worn on the seat that it was a wonder his ever-loving Jockey shorts weren't on display. Or maybe Murphy wore boxers these days. Maybe Murphy Jones had turned trendy and wore designer thongs. Like lottery balls popping into the air, wild, unpredictable, her thoughts slammed into each other.

He rested one plaster-dotted work shoe on the step below her and leaned forward. "Well, bless my soul. Look what the cat dragged in. And on a scorching June day. What brought you to this neck of the woods, Phoebe?" He nudged her bare knee with a long, callused finger, blinked, stepped back and crossed his arms.

"Hospitable as ever, I see." Laying her arm across Bird's shoulders, Phoebe smiled brightly up at him and wished desperately she'd found time for that red lipstick and that her feet weren't caked with dried mud. Fetching dimples would be a plus, too. "No how-do-you-do? No how's life been treating you in the last, oh, how many years has it been? Eight?"

He paused as if he were counting them up. "Yep. Eight sounds about right." The tip of his work boot nudged her bare toe. "Come for a visit, did you?"

From beneath the red and blue bandanna he'd tied over the top of his head and knotted at the back, damp, dark brown hair curled down his neck. A shine of sweat darkened his hair and skin, slipped down his temples to his jaw.

His glance slid to her daughter. The tiny bead of sweat vanished into the rumpled collar of his shirt. "Hey, kid," he said, nodding.

Frances Bird beamed at him, tilted her head and batted her eyelashes. Her rosebud mouth curled with happiness. "Hey, Mr. Man."

Phoebe almost sighed again, and stopped herself before she became a wind machine. Frances Bird had been born flirting. The result of an absentee father? Phoebe's own failure? Or simply southern genes asserting themselves in spite of an aggressively midwest upbringing? Phoebe tried not to overanalyze her daughter's lightning-bug sparkle around males. Tapping her daughter's shoulder, she said, "Frances Bird, meet my—what are you and I to each other, Murphy?" She lifted her chin, giving him a little attitude, but she couldn't manage the smile this time. "Not brother and sister."

"Not by a damn sight." Murphy held her gaze.

"Family, anyway," she said through a tight throat. "Family. That counts for something, even after eight years. Right?"

He didn't say a word.

"Hey," four-year-old Frances Bird said, her flushed cheeks dimpling with delight. "Me and my mom are going to live with you."

"Oh?" Murphy didn't move an inch. The pleasantly interested question would have fooled anyone who hadn't grown up with him.

But his poker-faced acknowledgment didn't fool Phoebe for an instant. She heard the dismay behind his affable drawl, and her anxiety increased, threatened to blaze out of control.

Avoiding his coolly distant perusal, she slicked Frances Bird's wet bangs off her face. "Well, sugar, that hasn't been decided." The worst he could do would be to send them packing. And if he did? She'd handle that, too. She had no choice. "We're here for an afternoon's visit. To catch up on old times. That's all. Don't panic, Murphy."

Bird's mouth puckered up with stubbornness. "You said—"

"I know what I said, Frances Bird." This time Phoebe couldn't stop the sigh that came rolling up from her toes.

"And what *did* you say, Phoebe?" A breeze lifted the corner of Murphy's shirt, brushed it back from his chest, died away in the stillness. "About coming to live with me?"

Frances Bird patted Phoebe's knees comfortingly. "Tell him, Mama, what you decided."

When Phoebe didn't speak, Frances Bird leaned forward confidingly and rested her elbows on her skinny knees as she looked up through her eyelashes at Murphy. "We are bums on the street. So we're going to live with you now 'cause we got no place else to go. And Mama said, home by damn—"

"Don't swear, Frances Bird."

"—is where when you go, they got to take you in. And that's that, she said."

"Yeah?"

With her hair swinging about her face, Bird nodded vigorously. Water dotted the faded blue of Murphy's jeans. "And, Mama," she said earnestly, "you say the damn word *all* the time."

Stifling the groan that battled with yet another sigh, Phoebe lifted Frances Bird onto her lap. "Shh, baby. The grownups have to talk now."

"That's for damn sure." He reached up and tugged at his bandanna, shadowing his eyes.

At Murphy's use of the forbidden word, Frances Bird poked Phoebe's face and rolled her eyes.

He studied them for a moment, a long moment that had Phoebe's bare toes curling and heat flooding through her again before he said softly, "Bums on the street, huh?"

"Not quite." Phoebe shaded her own eyes as Frances Bird leaped into explanation.

"Oh, yes. But we didn't sleep in boxes. We stayed at a motel one night. With tiny pink soaps. Soooo pretty. I kept one." Frances Bird batted her eyelashes again, smiled, and kept talking like the River Jordan, rolling right on down to eternity.

Phoebe yearned to sink through boards of the porch into a quiet, cool oblivion where Murphy Jones's too-observant gray eyes couldn't note her every twitch and flinch. Although easygoing, Murphy had never been a fool. Not likely he'd become one since she'd last had a conversation with him. This homecoming, if that's what it was, was not going well.

"We got fired, and we got debts, and—"

"Enough, Frances Bird." The hint of steel in Phoebe's voice finally silenced her chatty daughter. Lifting her chin, Phoebe held his gaze. "Well, Murphy, are you going to keep us standing outside for the rest of the night?"

He rubbed his chin with his knuckles thoughtfully. "Seems to me, Phoebe, you're sittin', not standin'." His drawl curled into the deepening blue twilight of the heat.

"Murphy's right, Mama." Frances Bird tugged the hem of Phoebe's shorts. "We're sitting."

She stood up. "Fine. Now I'm standing. Everybody happy?" Turning her back, she marched up the stairs to the swing, anger crackling down her spine with every mud-caked step. This was worse than she'd anticipated.

More humiliating.

She was tired, worried sick, and Murphy was only going to torment her, tease her, and drive her crazy the way he had when they were young. She'd never understood her reaction to him, or his to her, but she was in no mood today to sit or stand for it. Sherman had marched on Atlanta and burned it to the ground and maybe she was burning her bridges with a vengeance, but at the moment she couldn't care less if she left nothing but ashes in her wake.

And knowing his cool gray eyes were watching her every movement perversely fueled her temper.

She grabbed one of the battered suitcases and swung to face her daughter. "Bird, we're on our way. Say nice to have met you to Murphy." Wishing she'd pasted on that red lipstick after all, she stomped off the porch.

"Mama!" The frantic tug at Phoebe's shorts didn't stop her march down the steps. But Bird's anxious whisper, a whisper that was loud enough to hear from five feet away, halted Phoebe with one foot dangling in mid-air. "We got no place to go. You *said*."

"Come on into the house." Murphy's sigh echoed her earlier ones. Like chickenpox, sighing was apparently contagious. "Looks like that talk you mentioned can't wait." Metal jangled on the ring at his belt loop as he unclipped a key. The look he cast Frances Bird was shrewd. "Anyway, the kid must be hungry."

"*Very* hungry." With a lightning-fast mood change, Frances Bird smiled winsomely at him. "You got Jell-O? I like Jell-O. Red. With peaches."

"No red Jell-O." Murphy unlocked the door and flung it open. "Bananas okay?"

"I can make do." Bird dipped under his outstretched arm and into the dim interior of the house. "Mama says it's a skill us McAllisters got."

In the spirit of making do, Phoebe planted both feet firmly on the bottom step and reminded herself that she couldn't afford pride. Not today. Not tonight. Anger drained away, making room for the poisonous dread she'd been living with for weeks now. She met Murphy's guarded eyes and took a breath.

His wide hand rested on the door as he waited for Phoebe to follow her daughter. "Come into my parlor,'' he said, and the ironic edge to his low, slow words did nothing to settle the ping-pong bounce of her stomach.

"I know how that story ends,'' she muttered, dipping, like Phoebe, beneath his arm.

"Of course you do. You're a smart woman. And an educated one.'' The polite bend of his head toward her was even more unsettling as he shut the door quietly behind her. "But you came in anyway, didn't you, Miss Phoebe Fly?''

"Ms. Fly, please.'' She sent him a sweet smile as she scanned the room filled with cardboard boxes. Maybe she couldn't afford pride, but by heaven, she didn't have to let him know exactly how much the beggar maid she was. She trailed a finger along a dusty stack of boxes labeled CDs. "Love what you've done with your place. I guess the minimalist approach has a certain…charm to it, Murphy, but you've been here two years.''

He was so close behind her that his boots bumped against her heels, and she could swear his breath fluttered the hair at her neck. "Kept track, did you?''

"Same address on your Christmas cards the last couple of years.'' Hiding her dismay, she wandered through a maze of boxes toward the kitchen that she'd seen earlier through the windows. "No furniture?''

"Got a bed.'' His teeth flashed in a lazy smile. "Maybe I can't afford anything else.''

That smile had drawn the girls of their youth to him effortlessly. Murphy'd never had to work at collecting a string of shiny-haired, long-legged girls to him. Like bees swarming to the scent of flower honey, they merely appeared on the porch, beside his car, *everywhere.*

"No sofa. No TV. No chairs." Bewildered, she shook her head.

"Maybe I don't need much more. I'm a simple man, simple tastes." His smile widened until it lit up the gray depths of his eyes, sunlight flashing on bayou water, turning her knees to mush.

With an effort, she herded her thoughts together and forcibly drove memories back into the past where they belonged.

"Don't be irritating," she said. "Anyway, I can't believe you're too broke for furniture." Bending her head back, she examined the high ceilings, the crown moldings, and the heart of pine floors. Why on earth had he allowed this beautiful house to stay in such disarray for so long? "Murphy," she said as patiently as if she were talking to Frances Bird in a snit, "I know how much these old houses cost. And this one's in terrific condition."

"Did the work myself."

"Of course you did. But you're living like a man who's ready to pack up and hit the highway at a second's notice. You haven't even unpacked, have you?" Not bothering to wait for his answer, she sashayed through the wide arched doors into the kitchen and stopped so suddenly that he bumped slam up against her backside. "Oh, Murphy, this is beautiful," she whispered as she saw the light-oak pot rack suspended from the vaulted ceiling. Hanging above a work counter, the copper-bottomed pans blazed with light. "It's like the one—"

"In your folks' home." He stepped back, taking with him the comfort of his body against hers, leaving her desolate in a way she couldn't explain. But the kitchen, and Murphy next to her—the *rightness* of that moment overwhelmed her.

"Your home, too." She wouldn't cry. But the pots shone so brightly and familiarly, and she hadn't felt at home anywhere for so long. "Always your home, Murphy."

"Your parents were good people." He turned away from her and went to the industrial-sized refrigerator. "They gave me a…" he paused, his obvious discomfort painful to her.

"They gave you a *home*, Murphy. They loved you." She couldn't keep talking about her parents, about the past. Tears would make it impossible for her to do what she had to. "Mama and Pops loved you. You know that."

"Here, kid." He handed Frances Bird a black-skinned banana from the freezer.

"Cold." She poked it dubiously and frowned. "Why do you put your bananas in your freezer?"

Murphy scratched his chin, ran a finger under the edge of his bandanna. "Because they were going bad?"

"Okay." Frances Bird smushed the pulp out and into her mouth with a finger. "I like this." She beamed a wide, smeary smile. Dragging a stool up to the table in the middle of the room, she said, "And you can call me Bird."

"All right," Murphy said slowly, his voice whiskey-warm and smooth.

With Murphy's attention on Bird, Phoebe brushed the tears away from her eyes. Her gaze lingered on the table where Bird sat contentedly mashing frozen banana between her fingers.

Then, like an arrow piercing her, leaving her heart

aching, Phoebe realized why the kitchen felt so familiar. "You have the old table from home. From the
kitchen," she murmured, her palm sliding across the
smooth-grained walnut surface. She touched the ver-
tical dent where she'd slammed down the turkey
roaster in an argument with Murphy one Thanksgiv-
ing. If you could call it an argument when the other
person stayed as calm and controlled as Murphy always did. She traced the dent again. "You kept it."

"Pretty," Frances Bird crooned, running her hand
from one end of the table to the other, banana pulp
streaking behind her small hand. "Pretty, pretty."

Murphy's palm lay on the table across from
Phoebe's, his fingertips stroking the wood as if he
were unaware of his lingering touch against the grain.

"I needed a table. Your folks gave this one to me
when they bought the new one. The chairs weren't
salvageable."

"Oh." She looked at the two painted ladder-back
chairs lined up against the wall.

"I'm surprised you recognized the table. I refin-
ished it."

She swallowed. "I recognized it." Oh, she
couldn't, *wouldn't,* cry. Pain and yearning clamping
around her heart, she swallowed again, looking
blindly around the room that was like home.

Murphy didn't want to see the glitter in Phoebe's
eyes. She had no right to go all teary-eyed on him
over this damned table. It couldn't mean anything to
her.

She'd shaken the dust from home and town from
her heels, diploma in hand, and, as far as he knew,
never looked back. It had taken him hours to scrape
off the crackled varnish and sand the table, to find

the truth of the walnut. Every dusty, sweaty moment of sanding and stripping and scraping had been a pleasure. Compared to that, Phoebe's tears didn't mean diddly. *That* was a truth he needed to remember, too. He shrugged. "Just a piece of wood, that's all," he said, but his palm hesitated on the waxed surface.

"No." Her voice was low and husky with those tears. Mirroring his own motion, her hand moved slowly against the shining surface. "Not just a piece of wood. Memories." Her eyelashes fluttered, lifted, and for a moment he saw the tear-sparkle of her eyes.

"Piece of furniture. Needed repairing. That's all."

She turned toward him, almost as if she wanted to say something else, and her cheek caught the last ray of light from outside. He couldn't look away from the play of light against her skin.

Her face was as smooth, as glossy as the table's finish, as tempting to his touch. He'd learned the truth of that old wood, and he'd learned the truth of Phoebe. Like a butterfly, bright, fragile, she drifted here, there. Everywhere. As useless to expect that butterfly to last through the winter as to expect Phoebe Chapman McAllister to stay in Manatee Creek, to put down roots.

He lifted his hand carefully, his fingertips tingling as if he'd run them down a bare wire. Odd thoughts, this notion of Phoebe settling down, putting down roots. Tucking his palms under his armpits, he glanced at her with a scowl.

Her damp shirt clung to her like primer on drywall, every curve and bump outlined by the tangerine-colored, see-through cotton. He cleared his throat. He didn't need to be thinking about Phoebe's bumps and curves and how she looked like a juicy orange, all damp and glistening, waiting to be peeled. He tugged the bandanna from his head, wiped his hands and jammed the scarf into his pocket. "You and Frances Bird are wet. Y'all want to get into some dry clothes?"

"I'm *Bird*. I told you already. *Not* Frances Bird." Sitting on the stool she'd hauled to the table, Phoebe's daughter beamed up at him. "Unless you're real, real mad at me. Then everybody calls me Frances Bird." She patty-caked her banana-coated hands together. Bits of pulp spurted onto the floor. "But I will not ever, *ever*, make you mad at me and I will stay out of your way while we are living with you and not be a bother at all and I will clear the table and pick up after myself. Okey doke?" She slapped her hands together for emphasis.

Banana shot onto his chin, dripped to his clean floor.

"Frances Bird. Get a paper towel." Phoebe's voice was stiff, but he heard the anxiety in it.

"See? I told you how it is. Now Mama's mad at me." Bird wrinkled her nose and sighed heavily.

He thought he heard Phoebe sigh too as he said, "Don't bother, I'm fine. I'll clean up later. After your mama and I have our conversation."

"Right." The quick look Phoebe threw her daughter carried a message he couldn't quite decipher. Warning, sure. But something else there, too. The little girl settled back onto the stool, her brown eyes as big as paint-can lids. Phoebe shifted her feet, plucked at the drying fabric of her shorts where it stuck to her thighs. But she didn't say anything more even as her daughter wiggled on the stool.

Wiping his chin thoughtfully with the tail of his shirt, he examined Phoebe, seeing now the disturbing details he'd missed earlier.

Like the purple circles under her eyes, the tiny lines at their corners. Like the strain in her posture. Familiar but different, this Phoebe. He didn't quite know what to make of her, but he reckoned sooner or later she'd let him know what she wanted.

And sure as God made little green apples, Phoebe wanted something from him.

Her face was tense and her full bottom lip thinned with exasperation, but her eyes softened as she looked at her daughter. "Ah, Bird, sugar. I told you Murphy and I have to talk. We've landed on his doorstep without warning, I haven't had a chance to explain and—"

"And we're going to stay with him." The stool went in one direction, Bird in another, as she clambered down. "You said Murphy won't mind."

Phoebe was going to have her hands full in a few years with that little dickens. Maybe he'd let the heart-to-heart with Phoebe wait a bit. Murphy let his shirttail fall. No rush to find out exactly what she had in mind. Yeah, she and her daughter were turning his evening upside down, but Bird tickled his funny bone, he was hungry, and he was mighty curious to see how Phoebe was going to try and soften him up. No reason he couldn't let her play out her hand.

Taking his time, he smoothed his shirt down, and gave her a big grin.

Phoebe squinted at him.

"Taken to wearing glasses since I last saw you?"

She scowled, brown eyes darkening. "No, but I'm wondering why you're smiling like the devil's own son. You make me nervous when you smile like that, Murphy."

"Do I, Phoebe? How…fascinatin'. Never known you to be the nervous type before." He took a step toward her and noticed with interest that she didn't move an inch, but her scowl sharpened as he tugged at the edge of her almost-dry shirt, let the back of his knuckle graze lightly against the heat of her belly.

She angled her chin at him, letting him know he was mighty close to some invisible line and daring him to step across it. "Stop this, Murphy. You're irritating me. I told you not to."

He let his knuckle slide once more against that velvet skin. "Did you now?"

"Back away, Murphy." Brown eyes flared dark with temper and something else that made him lean into her, just that tiny bit closer, just to see what burned in those depths.

Phoebe had no idea how irritating he could be if he put his mind to it, and he was of a mind to irritate her, see what was behind her so-called spontaneous visit. Keeping his finger lightly wrapped in the brilliant cotton of her T-shirt, he asked, "So, you and Bird want to stay naturally air-conditioned or take a shower and change? Maybe stay for supper?"

"What are you up to, Murphy?"

He gave a tiny yank to the fabric. "Question is, sweetpea, what are *you* up to?"

This time he was positive he heard Phoebe sigh.

Chapter Two

The tickle of Murphy's knuckles against her bare skin sent shivers down to Phoebe's toes, and she inhaled with shock. She couldn't help it, didn't like it, didn't want to reveal how much the mere touch of him affected her, but the brush of his hand on her skin was so unbearably welcome, so terrifyingly right, that she knew she'd made an enormous mistake in thinking she could live in Murphy's house. Even for a week.

She couldn't.

And then she shook her head, clearing the haze from her eyes, and looked, *really* looked at him.

With each tug of his finger in her shirt, her skin prickled and jumped, but she realized that his teasing smile was that of the boy she'd grown up with, not that of a man intent on flirting. Not the smile of a man with seduction on his mind.

Embarrassed to the roots of her hair at her foolishness—this was *Murphy,* for Pete's sake—she smiled brightly, flipped her hair out of her eyes and told herself that she would manage somehow.

And she would keep a prudent, wary distance from Murphy Jones and his slow, easy grin that still turned her bones to pudding and her brain to mush. Heck, she could do that. She'd done it before. Now? It would be a snap, once she had a good night's sleep. Heck, she had experience, age and desperation on her side.

She would control her own silly reaction to him.

And she could manage Murphy.

Of course she could, she thought dubiously as she saw the tiny movement at the corner of his mouth as she flipped her hair carelessly, her very carelessness a masterpiece of acting.

"Me? Up to something?" She whirled past him, plopped on a suitcase.

"Yeah, that's the question." His mouth twitched.

"Why, what a suspicious mind you have, Murphy." She tossed him a grin, crossed her legs, and swung one leg up and down to the staccato rhythm pumping through her blood. "What with all your questions, a person might suspect you weren't thrilled to have her drop in for company." She slowed the gallop of her leg as his gaze followed its length, lingered along the top of her thigh, and moved on up to her face. It took all her effort not to yank at her suddenly too-short shorts.

"Don't forget. I know you, Phoebe," he said lightly. "And you're hopping around like a kid crossing hot sand."

"Don't *you* forget you haven't seen me in eight years. Maybe you don't know me as well as you think you do." She stood up so abruptly that the suitcase wobbled, thumped flat on the floor. Her heart was beating like a snare drum, and she was afraid she'd say the wrong thing and there wouldn't be a chance to salvage what she could from this situation that bordered on the disastrous. "People change, Murphy."

"Do they, sweetpea?" His face was shadowed by one of the pans hanging from the ceiling.

"Of course. It's called growing up. Maturing," she said, making her tone as light as soap bubbles. "We all go through it. Even me." She whirled away toward the door to the hall. "Anyway, I'll take you up on your offer of food and a change of clothes. Bird and I are bone-tired. A shower will be nice." Even knowing she was babbling, she couldn't stop the avalanche of words. "You have hot water, right? Hey, even a cold shower would be a treat after this heat. Golly gee, I don't know when I've felt this grubby and sticky, and I know you're ready for a shower after working in the sun all day, and Bird—"

"Phoebe. I have hot water."

Murphy's amused burr of a voice slid down her spine, silenced her. Oh, Lord, she was making such a fool of herself. She inhaled and scooted a suitcase toward Bird. "Open up, baby, and pick out your sleeping duds." Flipping open her own suitcase, trying her best to ignore Murphy's attentive gaze that was destroying her confidence with every tick of the clock, Phoebe crouched down and rummaged through carefully packed shorts and underwear. She finally grabbed blindly at the next piece of clothing that met her frantic fingers, something red and, she discovered too late, skimpy. With her best teddy clutched in her shaking fingers, she tried to shut her suitcase.

A long stretch of denim-covered thigh came so

close into view her eyes crossed. She shut them
against the splendid sight of muscles tightly wrapped
in faded blue. Murphy was in great shape. Terrific
shape. The quickly glimpsed shape of him burned
against her closed eyelids. Her face burned. She'd
swear even her kneecaps burned.

"Here." Two clicks and he'd closed the suitcases,
nudged them neatly against the wall with a dusty
work boot. "Easy does it."

"Right." She stood and puffed strands of hair out
of her eyes. Standing in one place, she jittered. She
needed action, movement. She needed escape from
the crazy turmoil of her feelings around him.

That was when Murphy's eyes, dark with pity, met
hers and the evening fell apart.

He'd taken her hands in his, and she'd wanted to
give up the effort, lean against him and bawl.

Later, oh, much, much later, she would remind herself that she hadn't thrown herself into his arms.
She'd kept her chin up even when his glance dropped
from her face to her hands. She could take pride in
that, and if a woman sometimes had to take pride
where she could, well, sister Suzie, that was life, as
her mama used to say.

Pride kept her chattering, filling the silence. A wall
of noise to keep the pity from his eyes. A wall to
protect herself from the unexpected urge to cry.

No matter what, she wouldn't cry. Not in front of
Murphy. Never, never, in front of him. That was
pride, too. Earlier in the day, she'd thought she
couldn't afford pride, but now she discovered she had
nothing else. In Murphy's kitchen with his guarded
gaze following her, his gray eyes taking in way too
much, she clung to pride.

He showered, returned to the kitchen and leaned against the wall, watching her, not saying a word. She chattered, she cooked, she bounced from counter to table and back again throughout a meal that seemed unending. And then, blessed relief, blessed escape, she bolted with Bird from that beautiful kitchen to the refuge of the bathroom and the comforting familiarity of bathing Bird.

Murphy listened to the sounds of Phoebe and her daughter giggling in his bathroom upstairs. Funny how this house, even as well insulated as it was, carried sound. He could almost turn the female hum into words if he listened attentively.

He didn't. He let his mind drift over the impressions of the afternoon and evening, trying to figure out the puzzle that was Phoebe. She was the same. She was different.

He recalled asking her, joking, but serious, too, what she was up to. In response, she'd tossed her head and hadn't answered him, but her pupils had expanded with panic for a second, or at least that was what it looked like to him, and then she'd smiled, brushed her hair back and turned away, his knuckle sliding against her skin.

But he'd felt the tension in her skin before she moved, that little ripple of muscles tightening, of the brain signaling alarm.

For a second he'd wondered about that tiny reaction. Been curious about that hitch in her breath and her deer-in-the-headlights expression. For just that second, he'd fought the urge to trace that smooth skin to the dip of her belly button. If he'd been a different kind of man, if he and Phoebe didn't have the history between them that they did, he would have cornered her then and there, pried the truth out of her.

But he'd never been a man who rushed anything, especially not a woman.

So, instead, he'd let an easy smile crease his face, he'd crossed his arms, and leaned against the table. Phoebe had flittered and fluttered from one end of the kitchen to the other, murmuring nonstop nonsense that went in one ear and out the other as he pondered her feverish activity and tried to see beneath all the flash and distraction she threw his way. Yawning, Bird floated in her wake, a small, sputtering tugboat.

Knowing Phoebe would continue in perpetual motion until she dropped in a heap, he'd finally peeled himself away from the table and moseyed over to her. He'd taken both her hands in his, stopping her agitated motions. The tension in her body radiated to him as her fingers trembled in his.

"Stop it, Phoebe. You haven't made a lick of sense for the last five minutes. I know you want something. Whatever it is can wait. I'm plumb tuckered out, and I've been working since before sun-up. Here's how we're going to play. First, we're all going to have a bite to eat. Maybe you want to give your daughter a bath and settle her down for the night. Then we'll see what's what."

"Right." She'd jerked her hands from his, spun away from him and stuffed her hands deep into her shorts pockets.

Too late. He'd seen the bitten-to-the-quick nails earlier. His gaze lingered on the hidden shape of her balled fists and he frowned. "Thought you quit chewing your fingernails when you were thirteen and started wearing Kiss Me Crazy Red nail polish?"

She'd flushed, stuttered into speech. "Bird and I'll figure out something to cook while you clean up from work. We'll eat. Bird will take a bath. That's what you said? Did I get it right?"

"Yep." He'd scratched his chin and tried to forget the ragged fingernails, their vulnerability striking at something inside him that he'd rather ignore. "See what you can find in the fridge. A sandwich. Anything will do. Like I said, I don't need much."

"Right," she'd muttered, letting her annoyance show.

He'd have to be dumb as a box of rocks to miss her annoyance. Nobody'd ever accused him of that.

He was secretly relieved, because an annoyed Phoebe was a million times better than a desperate, panicked one. "Oh, excellent, Phoebe. You've become a woman of few words. No long arguments. The world must be coming to an end." He lifted one eyebrow and sauntered out. He'd known without looking back that she'd watched him until he was out of sight. She always had.

Back then, when he was a teenager, truth to tell, he'd liked knowing she watched him. Liked seeing that shy pink rip over her face when he caught her looking.

Knowing her eyes were on him, he'd felt his pulse thump with an extra beat and been annoyed with himself. Thinking about that unwanted pulse thump, he'd stayed under the drumming lash of the shower until the water ran cold.

They'd eaten scrambled eggs with green peppers and onions and bacon, Phoebe chewing and swallowing with exaggerated pleasure, her hands in dizzying motion.

And then, balancing plates along her arm, she'd cleared the table and disappeared to bathe Bird while he cleaned up the kitchen. Phoebe had managed to use three of his new pans for her eggs. One for bacon, one for eggs, and one to sauté peppers and onions.

He would have used one pan. But that was Phoebe, turning everything topsy-turvy in a flurry of energy. He had to admit her cooking was better than his. Reflecting on this familiar but unknown Phoebe, he scrubbed and polished his pans, hung them back up on the rack, all facing in the same direction, and waited for her to finish putting Bird to bed.

He'd made a pallet of blankets and pillows for them in one of the empty bedrooms after opening the windows and turning on the ceiling fans. The stale, warm air of the closed rooms had moved sluggishly with the circling blades. He hoped the room would cool down as the night wore on.

For himself, he'd been in no hurry to install air-conditioning. He liked the rich earthiness of Florida's heat and humidity, but he wondered how Phoebe and Bird would manage with nothing more than the lazy pass of ceiling fans to cool them.

Outside the screened windows of the kitchen, he sensed the stirring of a breeze, heavy with heat, heard the tree frogs chirping in a mad chorus of another kind of heat. Outside in the darkness the air was pungent with the smell of summer and desire.

Inside, though, the air was honeyed with Phoebe.

He'd forgotten how pervasive the scents and sounds of a woman were. And Phoebe? Ah, Phoebe left a trail of sweet-smelling fragrance in his shower, down his halls, a hint of apples and oranges that had him breathing deeply in the solitude of his kitchen, and the sudden hunger gripping him owed nothing at all to the shining pots and pans around him.

The murmuring of their voices, the giggles, all the disruptive, intrusive sounds flowed over him, swamped him with sensations. Crowded him. Made him want to hightail it out of his own house. Nothing new there. Phoebe had always crowded him.

"Hell," he muttered, looking out the curtainless windows to the dark surrounding his house, a darkness that pressed in on him like the presence of Phoebe and her Bird.

Near the hall, a scarf, light and sheer, moved with some vagrant drift of air against his polished kitchen floor. The shimmering shape, all gold and red, seemed alive. As he stooped and picked up the scarf, the slippery material slid over the back of his hand. Lifting it to his nose, he breathed in the fragrance of Phoebe. More than bottled perfume, it was the scent of her, the very essence of her it seemed. The fabric caught against his end-of-the-day stubble, and he spread the scarf across the stool. That flimsy red thing she'd stuffed under Bird's clothes in the suitcase was enough to leave a man sleepless for a month. In an instant, before he could stop the thought, he'd pictured her in that tiny piece of fabric, her legs gleaming against the brilliant red, her hips curving under that blaze of shimmery material.

Feminine stuff, all these scents and sounds. Seductive, the silky, slippery textures of Phoebe's life.

He felt those invisible threads pulling tight around his chest, making his breathing shallow.

He didn't want those pictures of Phoebe in his head, in his dreams.

But something had driven her to his house.

He didn't want her here.

Not in his house, and for damned sure not in his well-ordered life. That was the bottom line. His life was finally under control, everything the way he liked it, thank you, ma'am. Bills paid. Business clicking along. Shoot, he didn't want to think about air-conditioning and whether or not he had acceptable food in his fridge. He didn't want to think about Phoebe's daughter's big eyes staring at him with awe.

He raked his hands through his hair, flicking the ends out of his eyes. Passing the stool where he'd placed her scarf, he let his fingers trail once more down that soft material. He didn't want all *this*. Silky scarves. Noise. Faintly perfumed air.

And Phoebe.

Lord knew he didn't want Phoebe Chapman— No. *McAllister*. He didn't want Phoebe by any name in his house, in his life.

But there was that little girl. Frances Bird.

He flattened his hand against the windowpane above the screen and the dark beyond it. Even to get rid of Phoebe, could he ignore that skinny kid with the big eyes that reminded him of Phoebe at that age? That kid who twinkled and dimpled and sparkled up at him like he was something special?

Him? Plain old Murphy Jones? He rubbed his palm flat against the glass. Yeah, that was something, the way that bitty girl had smiled at him. Could he really turn his back on her for no other reason than the fact that he and Phoebe were about as compatible as oil paint slopped over latex?

In the window, Phoebe's ghostly reflection watched him, blurred with her movement as she vanished.

He let his hand drop to his side and turned to face

his empty kitchen. At the front of the house, the screen door slapped shut, a soft, summer sound. He followed her out to the porch.

"Cooler out here," she said, sinking onto the swing.

"Your daughter all right upstairs?" He turned off the porch light, plunging them into darkness for a moment until their eyes adjusted to the night. "If she's miserable with the heat, let me know, okay?"

"Bird's fine. She fell asleep the minute her head hit the pillow. She's had a full day. She won't move until morning." She paused. Like pale birds, her hands beat against the darkness, disappeared behind her. "We're not hothouse flowers, Murphy. We can stand the heat. In or out of the kitchen," she added wryly. "I'm sorry. I made a mess of your kitchen, didn't I? You should have let me clean it up."

"You were busy."

In the dim light, he thought she seemed like a spirit that would vanish if he blinked. Or breathed.

Like pumping bellows, his lungs shuddered, whooshed.

Her bare foot rested on the swing seat, her chin on one bent knee. Barely moving the swing, she glided it to and fro with her other foot. In a cloud of curls her hair swooped forward, concealing her face, and with each slow movement of the swing, that apple scent carried to him. Her shampoo. She'd changed into clean shorts and a top the color of a house he'd painted last fall.

Ecru. Yeah, that was the color. No wonder she'd seemed ghostly, insubstantial in the windowpane. All that creamy white, like those pale night-blooming flowers with the scent that pervaded the summer nights and dreams of his youth. He couldn't remember the last time he'd smelled those flowers, but thinking about them now, he thought he caught a hint of their languorous scent in the air.

He folded himself into the wicker chair opposite her and waited, letting the night sounds and scents fill the space between them. For the first time since he'd driven up his driveway and seen her, laughing and drenched, joking—the butterfly girl he remembered—she was quiet. Diminished.

He didn't mind the silence. Silence was restful, easy. For long moments Phoebe nudged the swing in a hypnotic rhythm that came damned closed to lulling him asleep.

Would have, too, except that the flash of her leg in the night shadows would have kept a dying man awake.

And he was very much alive.

The firm curve of her calf flickering in the dim light with her movement entranced him. As did the push of her pale toes against the dark wood. Hypnotized, he couldn't look away from the shiny gleam of the colorless polish on her toenails as she flexed her foot.

"We used to sit out on the porch on summer nights. Remember?" She slowed the swing, shifted.

Her shape shimmered in the moonlight, and he wanted to reach out, grasp it. Hold it still. He tucked his hands flat under his armpits. "Yeah. I remember."

"Why did we stop?" Her voice was wistful and the hairs along his arms lifted, shivered.

"Like you said earlier, we grew up. We changed."

"You wanted to park on the fingers in the bay and neck like crazy with all those girls who tied up the phone line every night." The swing moved faster, stirring a swoosh of air around his ankles.

"Not all of them." Remembering some of those nights, Murphy felt a smile edging his lips.

"Oh?" The swing banged against the wall with her hard push against the floor. "I didn't realize you'd missed any."

"Keeping tabs on me?" Irrationally, the idea intrigued him.

"Not me. But I heard talk," she said virtuously. She curled both legs up onto the swing, let its motion carry her.

"No good comes of listening to gossip, you know."

She blew a raspberry. "You're the last person to try and play the saint, Murphy. That self-righteous air doesn't work for you."

"Ah, well."

Bent, her legs created mysterious shadows that dried his mouth. He shifted uncomfortably. "And you left for college. Didn't seem like anybody had time to drink lemonade and swing on the porch after that."

"You left first." She leaned forward, her hair catching the moonlight and trapping it. "You joined the army."

"College would have been wasted on me."

"Oh, Murphy, you could have gotten a football scholarship if you'd wanted. If you'd studied. Mama and Pops would have helped you in a second. You know they would have."

"I wasn't a student. Don't have the temperament for it. Sitting in class all day made me crazy. Anyway, it was time I left. Your folks were wonderful to me, but I needed to make my own way."

"Nobody wanted you to go, Murphy. You had other choices." Soft as a feather, her voice floated in the darkness to him. Across from him, her face was a shimmer of pale.

"Maybe."

He'd had to leave. He'd seen one too many moony-eyed boys hunkered down on the porch floor next to Phoebe while she laughed and giggled with them. Next to those lighthearted boys, he'd felt like an old man, their easy assumption of privilege foreign to him.

They had the right to come courting at Phoebe Chapman's door, and if the sight of them triggered a slow, treacherous burn, well, hey, tough for him. The Chapmans had given him everything good he had in life. He had no right to want more, to lie awake waiting for some hormonally overloaded Manatee Creek boy to bring Phoebe home from a date in his daddy's expensive automobile.

There would be the roar of a car up the driveway, the idle rumble of the engine, and then the motor would be turned off.

Silence.

And long, quiet moments while he waited for the slam of the car door, the bang of the screen door, her quick steps running past his bedroom door.

Of course he'd had to leave.

Years later in the army he finally understood that the scorn existed only in his mind. Those golden boys of Phoebe's youth had been only kids, some of them struggling like him. He was the one who'd kept his distance. Erecting a wall of toughness, he'd made sure no one got a chance to look down on him. That sense of being an outsider? It had all been inside him, not them.

He hadn't liked learning that truth about himself. Not at all.

"Why haven't you gotten married, Murphy? To one of those shiny-haired girls with the sexy voices? I kept waiting for Mama to send me a note that you'd finally done the deed." Her restless motion sent the swing careening to the side. "But you haven't." Soft, soft like her silky scarf, her voice brushed the air, trailed along his skin.

"I'm not a marrying kind of man, Phoebe," he said heavily, not liking the direction of the conversation.

"Not a college guy, not a marrying man. What are you then, Murphy?"

"A man who's comfortable with his life. Who likes what he does."

"You don't want someone in your life waiting for you to come home? The aroma of a good dinner cooking? Someone to share your thoughts with? You don't want any of that? You have everything you need?" There was distance in her voice, distance in the way she pulled back into the arms of the swing, and the poignancy in her tone. "But isn't there anything else you want?"

"Besides my pickup and my house? Reckon I could use a good huntin' dawg, sweetpea," he drawled, "but I don't hunt." He wanted her clever brain turning in a different direction, away from him and his choices. "Been thinking I might get a dog, though. Dogs are easy."

"Dogs need walking. They're pack animals. They like company. They're not *easy*." Again that annoyance rippled in her words. "And they sniff you."

He laughed. "A cat then. Shoot, sweetpea, I've known a cat or two that almost talked." He meant it as a joke, but the thought had been nudging him ever since he'd bought the house. He'd been thinking for a while it would be nice to have some warm, living creature waiting to greet him at the door, but a creature that didn't disrupt his life, didn't expect anything of him. "Maybe I'll get a cat, one of those big, old Maine coon cats. A guy kind of cat. Uncomplicated."

"That's the kind of life that appeals to you now? Easy? Uncomplicated?"

"Yes, Phoebe, it is." Leaning forward, he tapped her knee. "I like my life the way it is. I don't have to explain anything, don't have to apologize if I leave the toilet lid up, don't have to feel guilty if I stop off for a beer with the guys after work." He tamped down the slight melancholy that rose as he thought of all the nights he'd driven down the driveway to his dark house. "I can pick up and leave whenever I want to. I'm footloose and fancy free."

"Are you, Murphy?" Her solemn face was inches away from his, and her breath smelled of peppermint toothpaste, clean and tempting. "Really free?"

He leaned back. "Absolutely."

"And that's what you want? Absolute freedom?"

"That's it, sweetpea."

"Then why did you buy this house? Why have you put all that sweat and labor into making it beautiful? Because it is. It's a dream house." She rose to her feet and he did the same. "And that kitchen? Oh, your kitchen, Murphy." She clasped her hands in front of her, and her wrists brushed against his forearms. "That's not the kitchen of a man who's footloose and fancy free."

"That's the way it is, Phoebe." He couldn't bear the way her face softened, turned dreamy. Couldn't bear the drift of peppermint against his mouth. "But you've been asking all the questions." He grasped her hands with his. "So, enough about me. Like I asked you earlier, what are you up to?"

"Bird was right. We need a place to stay." Her hands jerked against his, but he held on. "For a week. Maybe two. Until I find a job."

"Why me?" The air closed in on him. "Why back in Manatee Creek, Phoebe? Because there's nothing here for you."

"Because I don't have anywhere else to go." Like a guitar string, she vibrated from head to toe, all that energy and emotion flooding him. And then she jerked her hands away from his. Her eyes fierce and mouth tight, her gaze scalded him. "Because I'm pregnant, that's why."

Chapter Three

Hands jammed into her pockets, Phoebe waited.

For judgment. For the thinning of Murphy's mouth that would reveal his distaste, waited for the words that would send her into the night with Bird and no hope.

She made her hands stay perfectly still. No matter what he said, she'd make a joke, she'd laugh off her announcement as teasing, she wouldn't let him see the terror swamping her. She'd lie, deny. "Gotcha," she'd tell him.

And then she'd run from Murphy's house as if the hounds of hell were growling at her heels.

She'd sleep in the bus station. She'd camp out in a church overnight. Surely churches in Manatee Creek hadn't started locking their doors at night? As much as it would kill her, she'd throw herself on the mercy of whoever found her in that church, a welcoming sanctuary she could almost see in her mind's eye.

No one would throw a pregnant woman and her four-year-old child out of a church, for heaven's sake.

Would they?

Well, there *was* that famous old story of the virgin and her child who couldn't find room anywhere except in a stable.

Jitters scurried like mice up and down her spine.

"Pregnant, Phoebe?" Murphy sat down in the chair, angled one leg over the other, and leaned back into the shadows. "Well, there's a surprise." His voice was as smooth and hard as polished silver. "I thought you and Tony were divorced. Who's the father? Not that it's any of my business, sweetpea."

"No. It isn't." Oh, she wanted the smart-aleck words back, yearned for the discipline to curb her unruly tongue. She didn't need to antagonize Murphy, not tonight, not with everything at stake. "Tony and I separated when Bird was two. I filed for divorce after two more years."

"A long separation."

"Yes." Her fingers curled tighter. She hadn't wanted the divorce. Divorce meant she'd failed, failure on such a sweeping scale that staying married and living apart was easier. "I...wasn't in any hurry."

"No?" That silvery voice and the rustle in the shadows were the only signs that Murphy was on the porch. "You must have wanted to get on with your life. Isn't that what all the magazines advise? Move on? Find closure? Where was your *closure*, sweetpea? Damn, I think you'd have wanted closure." His eyes glittered with anger. An anger that puzzled her.

"I don't know. I was busy. Time passed."

"Did it now?" Another rustle of denim and cotton. "Well, Phoebe, time has a way of doing that."

"As I said, I had things to do."

"Kept a tight schedule, did you?"

"I went back to college. Finished up the last three courses I needed for my degree and teacher certification."

"You were a busy little bee. Heck, finalizing a divorce must have been nothing more than some item on your to-do list. I can see how it happened." His voice was so understanding and compassionate that most folks would have missed the sarcasm icing it. The chair squeaked as he settled more deeply into it.

"The divorce wasn't high on my…to-do list, Murphy. It wasn't important."

But it had been. Everybody had told her she shouldn't marry Tony, but she had. Afterwards, when everything went wrong, she hadn't wanted to admit her mistake even to herself. And she sure didn't want to admit to anyone else that she should never have married him, that their relationship had been doomed from the beginning.

She'd become an adult.

Tony had stayed the same irresponsible, undependable youth she'd married.

"Strange reaction, Phoebe. To hang on to a marriage that was over."

"I had my reasons," she said stubbornly.

"Of course you did. You always do. Have your reasons, that is." An accusation she didn't understand in his hard tone.

She knew Murphy didn't want her and Bird disrupting his life. He was asking questions to shield himself from having to tell her he couldn't help her. He didn't have to spell it out. She could save them both that small embarrassment.

A mockingbird trilled suddenly, and she jumped, hurried into explanations. "All right. You want the story. Here it is. Ugly and pathetic and pointless. Tony showed up late one night in April, shortly before the divorce was final." Her breath was ragged as she remembered. "He just appeared. I was so surprised. He didn't phone or send a postcard letting me know he was in the area."

"No. Tony wouldn't have. That wasn't his style. To plan ahead." Murphy's gray eyes glinted in the light as he turned his head sharply.

"I just opened the door and there he was, soaked with a spring rain, laughing and saying he'd come to see his almost ex-wife before it was too late. For old times' sake. An impulse, he said. Maybe a reconciliation. A second chance."

Oh, she hated telling Murphy this part. Didn't want to. Would rather have walked over broken glass. Her failure still seemed so acute, even though she'd made her peace with it.

"But we'd had a hundred second chances, and they never worked out. I kept thinking I could do something differently. Change things. Hope's a sneaky old emotion, Murphy. It'll trick you every time."

"I wouldn't know. Reality's more my thing. A bird in the hand and all that."

She couldn't understand the edge in his voice, but she knew it was directed in her direction. Awkward, she hesitated.

"What happened next, Phoebe? After laughing boy rang your doorbell? Did you discuss a reconciliation?"

"A little." She rubbed her head fretfully. "And

Tony wanted to see Bird, too. He hadn't seen her since we'd separated.''

"Never managed to find the time before, I reckon? Being so busy himself?"

Murphy was jabbing, and she couldn't figure out why. His animosity seemed so personal, so cold-hearted. She fought the urge to defend Tony and continued. "He said this seemed like the perfect opportunity. But she was asleep. And I didn't have the heart to send him away." She rubbed her temples again and tried to ignore the stab of sorrow as she remembered Tony's laughing eyes sparkling in the rain, eyes that would never laugh again with such sheer pleasure at life's craziness. She swallowed. "I couldn't send him away."

"Because of the past."

"Because of Bird." Phoebe pressed her palms against her heated skin. How could she possibly make Murphy understand the events of that April night? How lonely she'd been and how sad for her daughter who was growing up without a father? She let her hands drop to her side. "But Bird never got to see him. And Tony and I, well—"

"A rainy evening. It was late. And Tony was...charming." Like silver coins, Murphy's words clinked between them.

"Tony was always charming." Her laugh spiraled into the night. "It was his birthright, that charm, that careless, happy-go-lucky, who-gives-a-damn charm. And that charm killed him."

"What?" With his sudden movement, the chair groaned again and Murphy's face floated in front of her, filled her vision. "Tony's *dead?* When? How?"

She thought for a moment he reached out to hold

her, and she was embarrassed to admit to herself how much she longed for that comfort, needed it. "Afterwards—the next morning—he went sky-diving. Early. An impulse. Before Bird and I woke up. He made a mistake."

"I don't understand." Murphy's face seemed blurred, foggy, and she blinked, trying to bring him into focus. "What do you mean, he made a mistake?"

"I guess I did, too. Three weeks later I discovered I was pregnant."

"Phoebe. What kind of mistake? How was he killed?" Murphy's palms cupped her shoulders, but his arms were so long, and he was so far away that she couldn't have leaned against his big, sturdy body if her life depended on it.

It was her bad luck that at the moment she felt as if her life and Bird's *did* depend on Murphy's strength and predictability, a predictability and solidness so different from Tony's mercurial, light-as-air charm. She wiped her cheek, surprised to discover the dampness there. "The April fool's joke is on me, isn't it? I'm the fool. Pregnant, penniless and pukey."

Murphy's astringent tone slapped her in the face. "Come on, Phoebe. Cut to the chase. You've never been a drama queen. What happened to Tony?"

Her head snapped up. Irritation cleared the tears from her eyes. Oh, she could see his tight, troubled expression as clear as water. "Right. He'd taken a video camera with him. He was distracted. He forgot to pull the cord on his chute. That was his mistake. And don't you *dare* say it was stupid, Murphy, or so help me—" Her hand rose into the air as if by its own volition, stopped an inch short of his face as he caught her wrist, his long fingers circling her wrist tightly.

"I didn't say it, Phoebe. You did. It's the truth. I know it. You know it."

"He's Bird's father. *Was*."

"And maybe he should have taken better care of her. Of you. Maybe he shouldn't have had his mind or his butt in the clouds. Maybe he should have been thinking about his responsibilities."

"Stop it, Murphy. You're being cruel. He's dead." She squirmed futilely in his grip.

"You're pregnant. He's not here to take care of you, Bird, or this baby either. Tell me again why Tony's behavior wasn't *stupid*—your word, remember."

He waited. Far off, an owl screeched. His words were the ones that had played over and over in her head, an unending loop of anger and guilt. How could she tell Murphy something she didn't believe herself? She couldn't, and so she stayed silent.

"The truth needs facing sometimes, Phoebe. And sometimes the truth *is* cruel." He stepped up so close to her that she could feel the heat of his anger burning against her. "Your mom and dad used to tell me some of the crazy things Tony did. They worried about you. They didn't want you to marry him."

"I know." She pulled her hand free and turned away from the accusing look in his eyes, from the confusing heat of his body. Her head throbbed with pain, lights shooting behind her eyelids. "I know. But *I* wanted to marry him."

"Because you were in love with him. Because you always got what you wanted. And so you dropped out of college and eloped."

"Yes. If you say so. That's exactly the way it happened." She raked her hands through her hair. "And I don't regret it for one second, Murphy, so don't think I do, you hear?"

"Oh, I hear you loud and clear, Phoebe." His hand shot out of the darkness and cupped her nape. "All's well lost for true love?" As if he weren't aware of what he was doing, he slipped his fingers through her hair, massaging, soothing the tight ache of her killer headache. "Right, Phoebe? He *was* your true love?"

She couldn't help the small sound that escaped her. "I loved him," she said defensively. "Of course I did."

"Did you, Phoebe?" He pressed the tips of his fingers against the coiled muscle at the base of her skull and kneaded. "I wonder."

Ah, heaven help her, the feel of Murphy's strong fingers working out the kinks in her neck, in her shoulders, the warmth of his hands against the pain, scattered her thoughts like dandelion tufts, and she couldn't think straight. "He was Bird's father, Murphy," she repeated through a haze of blessed relief that left her cooked-noodle limp. "I'd forgive him anything for giving me my Bird." Her head drooped forward as Murphy spread his fingers along her temples supporting its weight. "And I was to blame as much as Tony."

"I see."

She was afraid Murphy saw more than she'd meant him to, but it was too late. She couldn't take back her words. What did it matter if Murphy saw through to the emptiness of her marriage? After all, her feelings about Tony no longer mattered.

That long-ago anger and resentment because Bird

needed a father, and Tony couldn't fill that role? The anger at the waste of his life? Like a viper at her breast, that anger would have killed her. Would have destroyed her if she'd held it close and nursed it in the long, lonely nights after she'd left Tony.

She'd let the anger go and saved herself.

The guilt because she hadn't loved him? Ah, guilt lingered, corrosive and devious, a snake slithering through her unconscious.

She'd thought she loved Tony. But as for being *in love,* hoping that delicious, blinding rush of desire and emotion would substitute for true affection, oh, she'd soon learned it couldn't.

How could she blame Tony? Was it his fault that at best she'd ended up feeling nothing more than compassion toward him and occasional amusement at his silliness? At worst, exasperated and annoyed with his endless schemes and half-baked ideas?

No, that was her fault.

Because she'd mistaken lust and puppy love for the real thing. *There* was the stupidity.

She stepped back, away from the relief of Murphy's hands easing her pain. His touch lingered against her skin, warm, comforting.

At the same time he stepped back toward the railing of the porch. Casually he crossed his ankles, but he gripped the railing tightly, a puzzling tension in his careless posture. "So you came back to Manatee Creek?"

"Yes. Bird told you the truth. We had nowhere else to go. Will you let us stay until I can find a job? No longer, I promise."

Being Murphy, of course he had to gnaw at the bits of meat on the bone she'd given him, taking his own sweet time as he leaned against that dratted railing, watching her from the shadows.

Finally, surprising her by the direction of his thoughts, he said, "Since the divorce wasn't final, don't you have insurance money? A Social Security payout for Bird?"

"Ah, Murphy, please. Let it go." She half-turned, weary to the depths of her being. "It doesn't matter."

"I think it does." He snagged the back of her shirt, slowing her sluggish steps. "Why isn't there any money, Phoebe?"

She pulled away. Her shirt slipped out of his grasp. She walked toward the screen door, determined to leave. But then, her last shred of pride gone, she flung up her hands, swiveled to face him. "Fine. Here's your pound of flesh, Murphy. I didn't have enough coming in from Social Security to pay a week's grocery bill. Tony never managed to work long enough at any job that paid into Social Security. I used the ten thousand dollars from his insurance to pay for his funeral and to pay off his debts. He *owed* people. They needed their money, little though it was. There wasn't any left over. And I didn't know I was two paychecks away from being riffed from my teaching job. Maybe I would have handled things a whole lot differently if I'd known that. Okay? Happy now?"

"Delirious." He'd left the railing so fast she hadn't even been aware he was right beside her until he was just *there.* He slid his warm palm up the tense line of her spine, knuckling over each vertebra and smoothing out the muscles alongside her spine. "You're getting one of your headaches, aren't you?"

"Don't be nice, Murphy." Her throat closed. In

front of her, his shirt blurred again. "I can't take *nice* right now."

"Tough, sweetpea." He worked his thumbs along the base of her neck. "At the moment I'm in the mood to be nice. My turf. My choice."

"You're going to let us stay." Phoebe looked up at him, at his angular face dark against the black sky, and as he tilted her head back, tipping her chin to the stars, she could feel the bands around her head and chest loosening. "Aren't you?"

"Yeah. I reckon I am." Letting his hands drop, he poked her shoulder. "Go to bed, Phoebe. We'll figure out the details tomorrow. There's a bottle of pain medication in the bathroom medicine chest. Take one. Or two. And go to sleep."

Resting her head against the cool screen, she said, "I know you don't want us here. Don't want *me* here, Murphy."

There was silence in the darkness behind her.

She opened the screened door and went inside, walked slowly up Murphy's uncarpeted stairs, past cartons of packed belongings and into the bare room where Bird lay sleeping, her thumb tight in her rosebud mouth.

Tomorrow. Murphy had told her they would deal with everything tomorrow. And Murphy always kept his word. Always.

In the meantime, for the first time in weeks, she would sleep—deeply, dreamlessly.

She hoped.

With a blast of white-hot Florida sun, tomorrow crashed into uneasy, troubling dreams where Murphy kept walking away from her, his face hidden, his amused chuckle ringing in her ears.

And with a vaulting thump, Bird somersaulted onto Phoebe's chest. With her hair tickling her mother's cheek, Bird pressed her nose to Phoebe's and rubbed. She patted Phoebe's cheeks impatiently. "C'mon, Mama. Rise and shine. We got places to go and people to see."

"Oh, Bird." Phoebe groaned and buried her face in the pillow, away from the blinding sun and the bright face of her daughter. "No, baby. Trust me. Today we don't have to go anywhere. Later, maybe. But we don't have to do anything right this minute."

"Sure we do. We always have places to go."

"We're here, Bird. I'm going to look for a job. But not this minute. We're going to stay. For a while."

"Oh, good." Bird bounced on Phoebe's chest. "I like sleeping on the floor. I like Murphy's house. I like Murphy's yard. I like—" she crooned, beginning a litany that would go on as long as Bird could find words.

"Right." Phoebe sat up, dislodging her talkative child and tossing the sheet aside. "You like Murphy's everything."

"How 'bout you, sweetpea? Do you like my… everything?" Murphy slouched in the doorway, a cup of something that smelled seductively like coffee, good old shake-you-awake coffee—none of that decaffed, frappéd, foamed latte stuff. "Because I'm telling you, I sure do like your everything." His amused glance roamed over her shoulders, past the thin straps of the teddy she'd grabbed last night, lingered on her tingling breasts where her nipples suddenly budded tight and hard under the silk. "Oh yeah, sweetpea.

Your everything is in fine shape.'' He grinned. ''Want some coffee? It's decaf.''

She grabbed the sheet, clutched it to her, feeling heat rush from her breasts to her forehead. ''Yes. Good. Just, ah—'' She waved her arm carefully, easing behind the safety of Bird. ''Put it on the floor. Decaffed, huh? Okay. That's good.''

Bird, little flirt that she was, abandoned her, fled to Murphy. ''Hey, Murphy.'' She looked up at him. ''I like coffee, too.''

''You do?'' Murphy squatted, placed the mug of coffee on the floor, and with a provocative grin at Phoebe scooted it carefully in her direction and then turned to Bird. ''Well, how about me and you seeing what we can find in my kitchen?''

Bird took his hand as he stood up. ''Okay. But I can't start my day without my coffee.''

''Really?''

Phoebe groaned.

''Like mama, like daughter, huh?''

''I s'pose.'' Bird tugged at his arm. ''C'mon, Murphy. Let's go find what we can find.''

''Sounds like a plan, kid.'' Over his shoulder, he tipped his chin in Phoebe's direction. ''All right with you?''

''Oh, it's a splendid plan. Proceed. Immediately.''

Murphy stopped. Bird bumped into him when he turned in Phoebe's direction, his gray eyes letting her know he was appreciating every inch of what he could see. ''You okay, sweetpea? Not coming down with a fever, are you? You're awfully red,'' he said sympathetically. ''Sure would be a terrible thing for you to get sick.''

''No.'' Phoebe gritted her teeth. ''I don't have a

fever. I'm not sick. I'm perfectly fine. And I'll be even finer when I have a moment's privacy.''

"Oh, of course.'' He half-stooped to Bird. "Your mama always this cranky in the morning?''

Bird nodded and took his hand again. "Until she has her coffee. McAllister women need their coffee, you know.''

Phoebe pulled the sheet over her head. "Go. Now.''

"Mama'll be better after coffee.''

"I sure hope so.'' Murphy halted in the doorway, one hand resting on the doorknob. "Shame about your disposition, Phoebe. Enjoy the coffee. Even if it's decaffed. And the privacy.'' The rich darkness of his voice sparkled with amusement.

She knew, though, if she poked her head out from the sheet, she'd go hibiscus-red at the look in his eyes. He'd always been able to fluster her.

And clearly Murphy was on a mission to fluster her, to confuse her, to...? She didn't know. But something had changed in his attitude in those last moments before she'd gone up to bed.

"See you downstairs.'' The door snicked shut behind him.

Phoebe crawled out of the pallet to the coffee mug. Sitting cross-legged on the bare floor, she lifted the mug to her nose and inhaled the steam.

And moaned with pleasure.

Whatever devilment Murphy might have up his sleeve, he sure could brew a cup of coffee.

The door edged open again. Murphy stuck his head around the corner. "You okay? Throwing up or something?''

"I hate you, you know," she said calmly, inhaling the aroma again.

"Drink up, sweetpea. You'll like me just fine by the time you see the bottom of that mug. And speaking of bottoms, that red nothing you're wearing on yours is a treat for a hardworking man's eyes."

"This coffee is saving your life, Murphy, but don't push too hard." Phoebe sipped and felt warmth curl down to her toes. Or maybe it was the flash in Murphy's eyes that curled her toes. Whether it was coffee or Murphy, she felt like a kitten in the sun and resisted the urge to stretch with pleasure. "I haven't had coffee this good in a month of Sundays. I'd swear it had good ole pulse-pounding caffeine."

"Nope."

"Murphy!"

"I'm coming, Bird. Hold your horses," Murphy called down, but his gaze held Phoebe's.

His gray eyes were charcoal warm, a flame leaping in them. Her pulse fluttered frantically for a moment as he looked at her in the pool of bright sunlight. The hairs along her arms rose, tickling her skin with each second he stared at her. The thin silk of her teddy constricted her skin, stopped her breath as his gaze followed the narrow straps down to her breasts.

Her hand trembled and coffee slopped against the side of the mug. "Murphy, don't look at me like that."

"I like looking at you." His voice turned rough, dragged from some cavern deep inside him. He edged the door open a centimeter wider. "I can't help looking, Phoebe."

"But not like this." Her tummy tightened, bounced. "It's not—"

"How am I looking at you, Phoebe?"

"You know," she whispered, her throat going dry with a need that had no place in this house, no place in her life. A need she thought she'd outgrown.

She hadn't.

And the longer Murphy stared at her, his eyes dark with some emotion she didn't dare consider, the more she wondered how she was going to live in his house, live with him, for two weeks.

She'd thought she could handle Murphy.

She couldn't even handle her own feelings.

She clung to the mug with nerveless fingers, terrified by the force of the longing that rolled through her with the power of the moon on the tides.

"How am I looking at you?" he asked again. He took one step inside the bedroom.

Her gaze flew to the dark flush slashing his cheekbones.

Faintly, Bird's giggle rose from the kitchen.

Chapter Four

Murphy didn't think he'd ever seen anything as beautiful, as heartbreaking, as Phoebe in the morning sunlight, her hair rumpled and mussed, the soft skin of her cheek sleep-creased.

Exhaustion still smudged the fragile hollows of her cheekbones, shadowed her eyes. The morning light threw the purple half moons into cruel relief. Wanting to erase them, he stretched out his hand.

He'd no idea.

She'd hidden those signs of fatigue too well with makeup yesterday.

Sure, he'd seen the bitten fingernails, recognized the early signs of one of her paralyzing headaches. He'd seen the purple shadows under her eyes and thought they were the result of late nights and traveling. He'd even thought he understood her brittleness. But today in the harsh, unforgiving sunshine, he saw all the details evening and shock had kept from him.

Phoebe Chapman McAllister looked like a summer breeze would send her butt over teakettle. She looked like sleeping twelve hours a night wouldn't begin to bring back the natural color to her face.

She was holding herself together with the emotional equivalent of baling wire and twine. Through sheer grit and willpower, she was pushing her body to the edge of collapse. He could see it clearly now.

And he'd been a real jerk last night.

He'd been caught by surprise. He hadn't seen how strung out she was. He tightened his mouth in annoyance. No excuse. He couldn't give himself a pass on his behavior last night.

Fragile as blown glass, that was Phoebe this morning.

Nonplussed, he let his hand drop.

Because in spite of the air of fragility clinging to her like a faint scent, piercing his heart and his anger, there was Phoebe, the woman.

A woman he scarcely recognized after all these years.

This woman with wild, curling brown hair threaded with sunlight mesmerized him, stirred him. That silly red thing she'd slept in, a scrap of silk that revealed more than it hid, skimmed her curves with rosy color, transforming her into a glowing image of shimmering red and pearly skin, breasts and hips gleaming through the silk.

It was this woman who stirred him and sent the blood pooling in his groin.

And she knew.

Her trembling hands and dilated eyes told him she knew what held him at the edge of the room. The pucker of her nipples under the silk revealed what

she'd never say out loud. Told him that she was re-
sponding to whatever she saw in him.

Dangerous to stand here staring at her pale skin
flushed with red silk and something else, something
beguiling and feminine that called to the male in him.

Dangerous in ways he couldn't even imagine, not
with his blood drumming in his veins as he stared
into her eyes.

Dangerous because she was so frighteningly fragile, he could see that finally, and he couldn't,
shouldn't, wouldn't, do anything about the heat roaring through him.

Because Phoebe was in trouble and she'd come to
him for help.

Unnerving to feel the ache in his heart as his eyes
met hers and saw the courage he'd missed earlier.

And the desire.

He took a deep breath and held it, forced himself
to cast off the haze blinding him.

He didn't want to feel this surge of desire for
Phoebe McAllister.

And he sure as hell didn't want to feel this tenderness for a woman who'd walked out on her parents,
shaking the dust of Manatee Creek for her own selfish
reasons, not giving a second thought to the pain she
caused.

He didn't think she'd come home again except for
her parents' funerals. They'd needed her, he told himself righteously. And she'd abandoned them.

That was the truth that had always stuck in his
craw. She'd danced away, floating on the breeze and
out of sight like some bright summer butterfly. And
she'd left them behind.

Her parents.

Him.

It shouldn't matter, but it did.

He didn't know why. He resented her for that, too.

Wrapping her arms around herself, the mug of coffee tipping toward the floor with her movement, she looked at him with pleading brown eyes, eyes that sent a message different from her words, scattering his thoughts. "Murphy, please."

Was he wrong about her?

Had he misjudged her all these years?

He rubbed his eyes. Or, more likely, was he blinded by unexpected lust for a pretty woman in a piece of sexy red lingerie, caught unexpectedly by morning desire? "Yeah."

He didn't know what he was agreeing to.

"Right." She hugged herself tighter, a shiver of movement, and looked away from him. The angle of her chin dipped protectively as she curled into herself.

Footsteps clattered on the stairs. "Mama! Murphy! Come on!" Bird nudged at his leg, poked her head around him. "Whatcha doing?"

Murphy cleared his throat. "Good question, Bird. I got...distracted, I guess."

"Umm. Yes. Me, too." Avoiding his eyes, Phoebe sent her daughter a blinding smile. "You're hungry, aren't you, sugar dumpling?"

"Hungry, hungry, hungry." Bird bumped her shoulder against his thigh with each word and looked hopefully up at him. "Me and Murphy are going to scramble eggs this time, aren't we?"

He liked the confiding way she glanced up at him, rested her head against him. "Sure. Think you can stand a repeat of last night's supper, Phoebe?" He made himself smile and look at her as casually as he'd

look at a stranger, as casually as he'd look at any
guest. With an effort he made himself ignore the
shimmer of red silk. "Seems eggs are all I have in
the house."

"Come on, Murphy." Bird tugged at his hand impatiently. "With me. Mama's finishing her coffee."

"Yes, Murphy, you and Bird go ahead. Don't wait
for me." Phoebe's gaze hit the wall just to the right
of his head. "I'll be right down," she said in a stran-
gled voice. Leaving her face blotchy with color, the
hectic flush that had painted her from chest to face
was ebbing.

"Let's go, Bird." With a hand on Bird's shoulder,
he turned her toward the stairs. "Want to slide down
the banister?"

Bird stuck her thumb in her mouth, glanced toward
her mother.

Phoebe nodded. Red silk fluttered softly in the sunlight. "As long as you're with Murphy, it's okay."

The tightness in his chest loosened with her words.
He'd seen her protectiveness with her child. But
Phoebe trusted him with her daughter.

He didn't know why that mattered.

But it did.

Careless, butterfly Phoebe wasn't at all careless
with her child. That meant something, too, and he'd
think about it when Bird wasn't swooping down his
highly polished banister right into his arms.

She threw her arms tightly around his neck, latching onto him. "Catch me again, Murphy!"

"Sure, kid. Hike back to the top. I'll wait."

Bird stomped up each step, smacking her foot en-
ergetically against the wood. Upstairs, ah, up there,
he imagined he heard the soft sounds of Phoebe mov-

ing about the room, opening her treasure chest of a suitcase and rummaging among the stuff inside, tossing her silky red excuse for a nightie aside and changing clothes, sliding something cool and soft over the sleek curves of her legs—

"Ready or not, here I come!" Bird swooshed down, interrupting his X-rated thoughts, slid around the banister curve and back into his arms. "I love your banister, Murphy." She hugged him and gave his cheek a damp kiss.

"Good. I like it myself." He frowned down at her, not sure what to say next, not sure at all of what a kid her age would be interested in. Besides food. That much he knew about Bird. She liked her food. "Uh, you want to crack the eggs for me? Your mama let you do that?"

Bird gestured with a stubby finger for him to bend closer. "Yes. But I get shells in the eggs."

"I do, too. Sometimes. And I've been practicing a lot longer than you have, kid." He stood up, let her take his hand again, just as Rita Chapman had taken his hand years ago, when he was five.

She'd led him out of the grimy gas station where his mother had left him into a house with shining floors and meals on the table. She'd led him into a world he hadn't known existed.

That easily, without a second thought, Rita Chapman had taken him into her home, let it become his.

Through what means he'd never discovered, Rita had kept him out of the system. Even though the Chapmans hadn't been able to adopt him, they'd given him stability. A family. A father. And the Chapmans' year-old daughter became his baby sister.

He wished he could have believed it was his family. But he'd never been able to.

Maybe it was the blithe wave of his mother's hand as she'd told him to stay put and drink his soda pop. Or, perhaps, the lilt in her voice as she'd assured him that she'd be back shortly.

She hadn't returned.

No one had ever found her.

And he'd never looked.

He'd told himself he didn't need her, didn't want her.

He'd had the Chapmans. A family. Mother, father. A sister who wasn't. They were his family, not some woman and unknown man who'd abandoned him.

That belief was good enough for him. Everything clear and right, except for how he'd come to feel about Phoebe.

He remembered to the day when he'd forgotten to think of her as his sister. After that, no matter how hard he tried, no matter how ashamed he'd been, he'd never managed to feel brotherly toward her.

Some subtle, baffling shift had occurred, changing his relationship with her and leaving him on the fringe of their family, lonely and bewildered by the mess of emotions inside his adolescent self.

"Whatcha thinking, Murphy?" Bird pulled at the tail of his shirt. "You look like you ate a sour ball."

"I was thinking of when your mama was a young girl." He opened the refrigerator door and took out the carton of eggs.

"Was she pretty like now?" Bird climbed onto the stool near the counter and took an egg out of the container. "Because my mama is the prettiest mama in the whole world."

"She was…beautiful."

She had been beyond beautiful. Waiting for her date and his parents to take her to the Labor Day picnic, she'd stood before him in her turquoise two-piece swimming suit. Gangly long legs just beginning to take on curves stretched a mile and a half in front of his stupefied eyes. Pink and orange plastic seashells clipped her brown hair on top of her head. Bright orange toenails winked out at him from her flip-flops as she spun around, arms outstretched and a smile as brilliant as diamonds on her face.

Sweet innocence and siren all rolled into one small package.

She'd been thirteen. He'd been seventeen.

Too old for her sweetness. Too experienced for her awkward enchantress.

And too loyal to betray the couple who'd given him his life.

"Will he like me, Murphy, will he?" Spinning and spinning, her small rump a dot of blue-green in front of him, Phoebe had thrown her head back and given him her version of a sultry look from under the thick mascara of her eyelashes and the larded-on blue eye shadow. The tiny bumps of her breasts had barely made an impression in the stretch-knit top of her suit as she struck a movie-star pose.

Looking at her, he'd had a lump in his throat. His body went furnace-hot, and he had a sudden, intense desire to pop her fourteen-year-old, squeaky-voiced date in the face.

But he'd taken a deep breath, tipped her chin up and spat on the end of his shirt, moistening it. Then, carefully, even now he could remember how carefully, he'd wiped her face.

Her eyes were enormous, almost crossing as she watched him. The pupils were dark, huge, drowning him.

"Well, sweetpea," he'd drawled through that terrifying thickness in his throat, "Mikey'll sure like you better if he can see what's under all this goop." He'd scrubbed the mascara and heavy blue eye shadow off her face. "There. Yep, you're beautiful." And then he'd patted her on the head and said, "But don't let that punk get fresh with you. Smack him good if he tries anything, hear? Or come find me and I will."

"Oh, Murphy. Don't be silly." Scowling, she'd spun away from him, grabbed her beach towel and top and raced to the front door. "Mike's not a punk. He's on the football team."

"So?" he'd snarled, "Football players can't be punks? Since when?" But she was gone. Out the door on the first of a series of dates that kept the doorbell ringing and car doors slamming.

One of her clips had tumbled from her hair and he'd picked it up. He'd kept it and the shiny pink plastic was as bright today as it had been fifteen years ago.

Fifteen years. Before everything changed between him and his sister-who-wasn't.

"Uh oh." Bird held her hand out to him. Yellow yolk and white eggshells decorated her palm, dripped through her fingers onto the floor. "But I didn't get any shells in the bowl, Murphy." Trailing egg yolk, she held the bowl up to him. "See?"

He scratched his chin. He began to understand last night's disaster in the kitchen. "No shells, but not much egg in the bowl either. Crack another one. Let me show you."

Ten eggs later, Murphy decided he and Bird had enough eggs in the bowl for breakfast.

Bird was a nonstop talker, a constantly moving whirl of energy. He wondered for a moment how Phoebe managed.

Moments later, she strolled through the kitchen door in a glow of yellow shorts and tangerine blouse and showed him how she did it. Moving quickly, she washed Bird's hands, tied a dish towel around her like a bib, and paper toweled up the mess. And all the while, she dipped and moved and arranged.

And she talked, a stream of shiny words flowing from her like water racing over stones.

He began to see where Bird had inherited her conversational style.

Makeup glossed her face, hid the shadows, gave an illusion of energy and vibrancy.

But he'd seen Phoebe's morning face, and he wouldn't forget that fragility anytime soon.

"I thought you started work early, Murphy." Phoebe popped two slices of bread into his new toaster. "Bird and I are messing up your schedule, aren't we? Look, you go on with your plans. I'm sure you have work lined up for today. Do what you have to. We'll manage. Right, Bird?"

"Right." Bird spread orange marmalade over the strips of toast Phoebe had cut for her. "McAllister women are good at managing." She folded the strip into a fan and tucked it into her mouth. Both cheeks puffed out like a chipmunk.

"I called and said I wouldn't be at work until noon. Everything's fine, Phoebe."

"Okay. Good." She collapsed into the purple kitchen chair, immediately leaped up and raced to the fridge. "Milk." She filled three glasses and set them on the table. "Nice glasses, Murphy."

"Grocery store giveaways. A promotion. I needed glasses. Seemed like a good deal at the time." He fingered the outline of virulent green cabbages on the glass he held. "And a reminder to eat your vegetables."

"I like peas. But I like them frozen, not cooked." Above the rim of her glass with its lineup of never-before-seen-in-nature-orange carrots, Bird's eyes met his.

"How did you manage to make your way here, Phoebe?"

She set her glass on the table, shifted it to her right. "We flew in from Wisconsin."

"And we took a shuttle bus and a cab with a nice man who knew 'zactly where you live, Murphy. How did he know that?"

Turning to Bird, he said in his most serious tone, "Everybody knows me. Didn't you see the signs with my name on them at the airport?"

"Maybe. But I don't know how to read your name. I can read some words. And I know my address and phone number and—" Her forehead wrinkled as she studied him. "You're making a joke, aren't you?"

He grinned. "I am."

"I like jokes." She grinned companionably back at him.

He heard Phoebe's knife clatter on the table. "Bird likes everything."

"I don't like liver."

"I don't either." Murphy made a mock shudder. He was beginning to get the hang of conversing with women of this age. He tugged a strand of Bird's hair and mock-shuddered again. "And I hate ice cream."

Bird's thin face scrunched up. "I sure hope you're making a joke."

"I am."

She nodded once, emphatically. "That's what I thought. Me and you are jokers, Murphy, aren't we?"

His nod echoed hers.

"Besides, everybody likes ice cream. You can come to my birthday party and have ice cream. Napoleon. Because it has all three of my most favorite flavors."

"I like Napoleon, too," he said, copying her pronunciation. He leaned back in his chair. "So, Phoebe, what do you want to do today? Go on a search for Napoleon ice cream?"

"Look for a job." Phoebe jerked to her feet and began cleaning off the table. Her forehead pleated. "That's right up there on my to-do list, let me tell you."

"Sit down, sweetpea. No wonder your eyes look like you're first cousin to a raccoon."

Bird sputtered milk onto her chin. "My raccoon mommy."

"I haven't seen you sit still for more than five minutes at a stretch."

"I have—"

"Places to go and people to see," Bird chimed in. "We made plans, Murphy, before we came to live with you. Mama didn't want to wake up, and she said we didn't have to go anywhere today, but we do. We got no time to waste because me and Mama are going to have a baby in a little while, you see."

Phoebe's sigh rolled up from her toes. "Damn."

"See how it is, Murphy?" Bird rolled her eyes. "Mama won't swear when the new baby comes, though. Me and Mama will have to be 'zamples for the baby."

"All right. That's enough, Bird. My plans, Murphy? Simple, really. No biggie. I intend to go job-hunting today. Find an apartment. Apply for my Florida teacher's certificate. Check out what kind of credits I'll need, find out if I'll have to take extra courses to qualify for Florida. And then I have to stop at a bank and arrange—" She stopped. "Anyway, I have a lot of errands."

"What about Bird?"

"Bird goes with me."

Bird squirmed on the seat. "McAllister women—"

"Stick together?" He finished the sentence before Bird did.

A faint smile touched Phoebe's mouth. "You learn fast."

"Yeah. I'm learning a lot about—"

"McAllister women?" This time Phoebe finished the sentence for him. Her smile tilted the corners of her mouth. "Oh, we're deep, we are. And complicated." She grimaced, then stood up quickly.

He snagged her arm, tugging her back into her chair. "Patience, Phoebe."

Her scowl deepened. "Sounds as if you're naming a singing group. You know, Patience, Phoebe and Patty."

"You couldn't carry a tune in a bucket, sweetpea." He snickered. "Remember? I knew you when." Teasing was safe, a refuge for the conflicting feelings romping around inside him.

Tenderness and lust could turn a man inside out.

Bird propped her elbows on the still sticky table and leaned toward him. "What does that mean, Murphy? When did you know my mama?"

"Your mama and I have known each other most of our lives. We grew up together. Your grandma and grandpa raised me."

"Then why aren't you Murphy Chapman like Mama was?" Bird rocked on the chair. "I don't understand."

"Bird, enough questions." Phoebe's quiet warning didn't even slow Bird's torrent.

"They're your mama and papa, too? You're Mama's brother?"

Phoebe's leg jerked under the table. She went very still.

"No," he said.

Bird dug her finger into her chin, puzzlement twisting her face. "Where are your mama and papa?"

He didn't know how to answer her guileless question. Almost anything he said would make the situation uncomfortable. And what could a little girl like her understand, anyway? "I don't know," he said finally, opting for truth.

"I don't got a daddy." She rested her head on her folded hands. "But I got my mama. You don't got a mama, Murphy?"

"No. Not really." How could he explain the complicated love he'd felt, still felt, for the Chapmans?

He'd tried hard not to think of their kindness as merely casual charity, but he'd been so aware, even at five, of what his life would have become without them. Even though they'd treated him like a son, he'd never truly felt a part of their lives.

Maybe he'd been too old by the time Rita rescued him.

Or maybe it was his own nature that kept him on the outside, looking into the windows of other people's lives.

"I know a boy who has six uncles. Are you my uncle?"

"No, Bird, I'm not." Murphy resisted the urge to look to Phoebe for help. He wanted to answer Bird's questions in spite of his growing discomfort. But how in hell did parents know what to say? Did hospitals hand out a book of instructions bundled up with the babies they sent home? Did parents latch onto some guide book to help them through the thickets of questions like Bird's? He raked his hands over his hair. "Uh, your grandma and grandpa raised me, but your mom and I aren't brother and sister."

"Okay." She bounced her chin on her hands. "Then are you one of my cousins? Mama said I had second cousins in Florida."

"No. I'm not even a cousin."

"I am very confused. I do not understand at all. Who are you, Murphy?" Bird screwed up her mouth.

"Damned if I know." An old pain made his words sharper than he meant them to be. "I'm...just Murphy, that's all."

Bird studied him for long seconds. Finally, laying her small palm flat on his hand, she said, "You can be *my* Murphy, that's who you are."

He turned his hand palm-up and grasped her hand. A curious tickling in his throat made him cough. "I'd be honored to be...*your* Murphy."

"Well, of course. Because everybody's got to have

somebody. Now you belong to me." She closed her fist around his thumb. "Okay?"

"Okay," he said. The feel of her small hand clinging to his turned his heart over.

The thought sneaked into his head as Bird kept her hand in his—Was this how Rita Chapman had felt that long-ago day?

Suddenly the past seemed glossed with a different tint, a shade that changed things.

Because *charity* didn't begin to describe the rush of emotions swirling through him as Phoebe's daughter looked at him steadily with her trusting, innocent eyes.

Chapter Five

The fleeting glance Murphy gave her was filled with such sadness and loss, with such piercing loneliness, that Phoebe held her breath.

As if a curtain had parted before her, she suddenly saw through the mist, clearly, for the first time.

And then he blinked, looked toward Bird, and the expression was gone, an illusion of light and shadow.

Phoebe decided the shuttered, haunted look on Murphy's face had come from Bird's persistent questioning, or from the upheaval they'd caused in his life.

Or possibly from the rubbery eggs speckled with shell.

But she couldn't forget that glimpse of a Murphy she didn't know, that sense of a man filled with an enormous sadness. Like a thin veil, that moment shaded her perception of him, blurring the landscape of her memories.

"Bird," she said gently, "Murphy has to go to

work. Finish your toast and juice. We can't pester him with one question after another.''

The brilliance of Bird's smile would have shamed a tray full of jewels. "My Murphy doesn't mind, do you?"

Tranquil, amused, Murphy's gaze met Phoebe's. "I don't mind questions.''

She'd been mistaken and the relief was incredible. She didn't want to think of Murphy filled with loneliness and sadness. "Still, Bird, too many questions are rude.''

Bird scowled. "I don't care. My Murphy knows I got to understand things. That's silly, Mama. How will I understand if I don't ask questions?"

"Kid's got a point." Murphy's angular face had returned to its usual impassivity. "And she needed to figure out what slot I belonged in. Because you hadn't explained, had you, sweetpea?" A tiny, barely perceptible resentment surfed along the top of his words.

"We didn't have a lot of time to catch up on old history, Murphy, before we left Janesville.''

"Oh? I didn't realize your decision to relocate was an impulse.''

"Not an impulse. But a quick decision." She gripped the edge of the table to keep from leaping out of the purple chair and to her feet, to keep from moving around Murphy's sun-filled kitchen.

"The baby?" His gaze lingered on her belly.

"Yes." She couldn't sit any longer. Lining up plates along her arm, she headed for the sink. "Murphy, can you give us a lift into town? I'll arrange to rent a car for a day or two until I find a job, and then I won't have to bother you again.''

"You're planning on renting a car?" His gaze sharpened. "Expensive idea."

"I know." She smiled and poured soap powder into the container in the dishwasher. "Not a problem."

"Thought you said you were broke?"

"I am." Still smiling for all she was worth, she closed and latched the dishwashing machine. "But my credit card has a little room left on it," she lied. It didn't. She'd bought groceries with it until she'd maxed her limit. "You've given us a place to stay. We can manage now."

"That's what you keep saying. Why don't I believe you?" He followed her to the table, his work boots nipping at her heels.

"Because you never take anything at face value?" She whipped the dishrag past his nose and briskly wiped the table. "Anyway, Murphy, we're not your problem. You've done enough by letting us invade your new home."

"I couldn't have sent you away, Phoebe. You must have known that. Or else why make the trip to Manatee Creek?" He turned a kitchen chair backwards and draped himself over it.

While he stayed that nice, safe distance away, she hung the dishcloth over the faucet. Then, keeping her back to him, she took the clean skillets and walked briskly toward the hanging rack. Reaching up, she hung the small skillet on its hook. "You didn't have to take us in. Not on my account."

Murphy stood up, hung the heavier pan and sat back down. "Maybe not. But you're wrong. I did have to. Because of Rita and Bannister."

This was the fear that had kept her from running to Murphy sooner than she had.

She despised the idea that he would help her out of obligation. The idea that he would see her as an object of pity made her skin crawl. "You don't owe me anything because of Mama and Pops."

"Of course I do." Shoving his chair back, he stood up and was suddenly *there,* beside her, one hand cupping her shoulder. Rasping her skin, his brown, callused fingers bunched the thin cotton of her blouse. "How could I turn you away, Phoebe? What kind of monster do you think I am?"

"My Murphy's not a monster, Mama." Bird looked up from the trail of teeny paper balls she was lining up along the far wall.

"Of course not, sugar plum." Pivoting to face him, Phoebe lowered her voice. "Murphy, you know I don't think you're a monster." She clasped her hands in front of her to keep them still for a moment. How could she make him see how hard taking his charity was for her? "Look, we haven't really seen each other in eight years. At best we've exchanged cards, the occasional letter. You were in the army. You couldn't get home in time for either Mama or Pops' funerals. What can I say? We've lived separate lives." Holding her hands tightly together, she said, "The only time we've talked on the phone was to make arrangements for the sale of the house after Mama's funeral."

"And why do you think that was, Phoebe? That we...lost touch with each other?" His expression conveyed nothing more than polite interest.

"I don't have a clue," she said desperately. But she knew, oh, she knew.

"After you left for college, you never came home again, Phoebe, did you?"

She wouldn't, couldn't, tell him the humiliating truth. But her mother had guessed—and remained silent over the years.

"You should have."

She thought she heard a faint accusation in his voice. Not understanding it, she ignored it. Hurrying back to the sink, seeking refuge in action, she concentrated on polishing its stainless steel surfaces until the whole room and her agitated face shone back at her.

She saw Murphy's face, too, in the shining surfaces as he came right after her.

She couldn't ignore his presence at her back, the warmth radiating out to her, the shift of his thigh muscles against the backs of her bare legs as he waited for her to respond.

She definitely didn't want to get into the complicated reasons why she made a point of avoiding Murphy and Manatee Creek after leaving for college. That would open a can of worms she didn't have the time or energy to deal with. Not now, maybe never.

Reaching around her with both arms, Murphy flipped the cold-water lever. The hairs along his corded forearms brushed against her wrists. "Thought you needed some water to rinse away all that soap. Think the sink will survive all this scrubbing, Phoebe?"

Trapped between his arms, she tucked her elbows in close. The dishwasher vibrated under her hands. Dimly she sensed that to touch him even accidentally would be disastrous. It would open some door she'd slammed shut long ago.

Freeing her, he stepped away. With his movement, a current of air eddied around her, stroking the backs of her calves and her thighs.

Grimly, she wrung out the dishrag, twisting it so tightly her fingers hurt.

Murphy was the reason she'd fled home, gratefully escaping to college. For a long time she'd kept herself busy. Marriage. Motherhood. Earning a living. The problems with Tony.

Those uncomfortable, bewildering feelings that had sent her running from Manatee Creek and Murphy disappeared under the weight of daily life.

She hadn't had time to think about Murphy during those years.

Not really.

Not often.

But still, some tiny, self-aware part of her subconscious had made sure that she stayed out of Murphy's space.

It was her bad luck now that his space had become the only place.

Under the circumstances, she sure as heck didn't want to resurrect that jumble of adolescent feelings.

Nope, the subject of why she hadn't come home until now wasn't one she and Murphy should bring out into the open.

Whatever accusation he was throwing at her could wait for another time.

Or be skipped altogether.

After all, how long would she be underfoot? She'd said two weeks. She might find a job sooner.

If she did—and, oh, she entreated heaven and whatever gods were on duty that she would—then she and Bird would be out of Murphy's house. Out of his life.

They could all go on as before. That was what she wanted. Wasn't it?

She finished drying the sink. Not finding anything else to wipe, dry or polish, she steeled herself against those tingles that ran over her skin every time he came within a foot of her, and approached him. He'd propped himself against the wall opposite Bird's industrious trail-making. His eyes held hers as she walked toward him and she stopped short, choosing instead to sit down.

"Murphy, what I want to say is that Mama and Pops aren't here anymore. We're really not a family. I'm not your responsibility. How in the world could I expect you to—"

"You think I could take everything your mom and dad gave me and then refuse to give their daughter a port in a storm? You have every right to ask me for help. Hell, you should have demanded help."

"Demanded?"

"That's your *right*. You know I'd do anything for them. In their memory." One long stride brought him back to her, crowding her where she sat.

Sitting down had been a mistake. She crossed her arms and leaned as far back as she could. She said, "Demands aren't the best way to convince someone to do a favor for you. Not in my experience, at least."

He bent his knees, stooping, until they were eye to eye and she had nowhere else to look except into the stormy depths of his gray eyes. His knees bumped hers. "Well, the past, as they say, is history and not important right now. But the truth is, we shared that history, and, like it or not, sweetpea, I'm what's left of your family. And I reckon you've just insulted me."

"Oh, Murphy. I didn't mean to insult you." There was no way to run past him, no place to turn. She was face to face, knee to knee with him, his chest blocking her view. "But I don't want to be an obligation either."

"What I don't quite get, Phoebe, is that you say you didn't feel you could ask for my help, but you came looking for it anyway. Can you explain that to me?"

Curling her bare feet under the chair rung, she let her head droop forward, escaping the intensity of his presence. "I didn't have any choices left. Nowhere else to turn."

Behind them, Bird murmured to herself.

"Didn't you? That's surprising. You must have had other solutions. Other…friends."

"I…just acted without thinking the situation through. That's all."

Go home to Murphy. That's where you'll be safe. The words had appeared in her brain like a message, and she'd packed up and headed for Florida.

"Look, I don't think of you as an obligation." He stood up and walked to the window.

Like a marble statue the long indentation of his back was sculpted with muscle definition even under his T-shirt, a lure to her sense of touch. He crossed his arms and the T-shirt tightened, delineating the broad bands of muscle across his shoulders.

Murphy didn't have a gym-toned body. Radiating a power and force that derived from hard work, his body was more imposing because of the sense of purpose behind the muscles, behind the power. His shoulders hunched. "You're not a…charity case, Phoebe."

"But I am. That's the bottom line."

"You're wrong. That's not the case. So put your mind at ease. I know I didn't throw you a welcoming party yesterday, and I apologize. It's not an excuse, but you caught me by surprise."

"I know." She didn't want to bring up the subject of how he must hate the invasion of his life. Not in front of Bird, she didn't. Bird heard too much as it was, and she'd had enough confusion to last her for a long time. Bird liked Murphy. She didn't need to think he didn't want them there.

Murphy would make the best of the situation. She supposed she'd known that, too. Had counted on it. And that was the real answer to Murphy's question.

She'd hated having to count on him to rescue her.

And she despised that part of her deepest self that wished he would say he was happy she and Bird had come to him.

That realization was the most humiliating of all.

Still not looking at her, shoulders still hunched, he added, "Here is where you need to be. Where you should be. Bird was right. Home is where you're supposed to go when you need to. You needed help. You made the right decision."

"Fine. Thank you." She gripped the edge of the table.

He turned, and the light pouring in from the window hid his expression. "You said you want a ride into town?"

"Yes. Absolutely."

"If you're sure that's what you want."

"I am."

He paused before saying slowly, carefully,

"Wouldn't it be better to take today and rest? Sort out your plans?"

Loathing herself for even considering his offer, she hesitated. The very idea of a whole day where she didn't have to do anything, didn't have to cope, was temptation beyond fairness.

She hoped the bank deposit from the car dealership in Wisconsin showed up in her Janesville account. She'd been told it would take a week to clear. If it had cleared, she would have five hundred dollars from the sale of her junker car to last her until she landed a job.

She hadn't trusted the car to make the trip from Wisconsin to Florida. And she wouldn't risk Bird that way, risk stranding them on some long, empty stretch of road with no money and no resources. Her hands shaking as she filled out the withdrawal slip, she'd emptied her account of the money from her final paycheck and bought the cheapest plane tickets she could find.

Running her fingers along the edge of the table, she considered the possibilities. Until the car dealer's check cleared, she was dependent on that fifty dollars tucked away in her purse.

She had no intention of filling Murphy in on those minor details. He knew more than enough already.

Reaching a decision, she rose and walked over to Bird. What a treat, a gift, it would be to spend the day playing with her daughter, not *doing* anything, simply *being*. The stab of longing to spend the day doing exactly that caught her by surprise. Stooping down, she nudged Bird's line of white balls. "What are you making, sugar plum?"

"A trail for Hansel and Gretel." Bird turned the

corner cabinet and continued down the length of the
kitchen. "So they can find their home and their mama
and papa."

"Oh." Phoebe stood up and dusted her hands off
emphatically. "Thanks for the advice, Murphy. But I
really can't afford to waste the day." She couldn't
believe how hard it was for her to turn away from the
delicious luxury he dangled in front of her. He
couldn't possibly realize how tantalizing his suggestion was. How tired she was.

"Fine." A set of car keys jingled against the
counter. "But use my car. There's no sense in splurg-
ing on a rental."

She could do that. If she used Murphy's car, she
could save those last dollars for an emergency. He
offered her a way out of her immediate dilemma so
easily.

But....

The road to hell was paved with easy decisions like
this. What would she do if she wrecked his car? Dam-
aged it? Her thoughts running to the worst of scenar-
ios, she shuddered. "Thanks, but no thanks." Wistfully, she edged the keys, so shiny and cool and
tempting, back in his direction.

"Don't be an idiot, sweetpea. The car's sitting
there. I use the truck. Why rent a car when there's a
perfectly good vehicle in the garage?" He lifted the
keys and plunked them into her hand, closing her fingers around them when she tried to pull her hand
away. "And I don't have time to run you into town
anyway. My job's at the other end of the county."

"You're lying, of course." She'd heard the lie in
the lightness of his voice.

"Maybe." He grinned at her. "But what difference

does it make if I am? What's the big deal about using my car? It's in the garage, doing nothing except collecting dust.''

"I don't like borrowing other people's things,'' she said doggedly, feeling cornered in some indefinable way.

"Don't be so stubborn. And if you wreck the damn thing, the insurance will cover it.''

"What?'' She stopped so abruptly that she tilted forward.

"Yeah, I know what you were thinking. But don't worry. The car's only metal and plastic. If it breaks, hey, it's fixable.'' His eyes narrowed on her as he waited. "I don't understand why you're turning a simple situation into something complicated. Now, are you going to do the sensible thing or not?''

The cool, serrated metal edges of the keys bit into her palm. One key, smooth plastic, was a remote car door opener.

A key to a car she didn't have to pay for.

Where was the harm except to her pride? And hadn't she already sucker-punched that poor pride of hers into oblivion? Why strain at a gnat when she'd already swallowed the camel?

"Or,'' Murphy's voice slid into a lower register, a challenge in it as she flipped the keys in her hand, "are you going to be stubborn, pigheaded, and ornery?''

If she used Murphy's car, she reminded herself, she'd have the fifty dollars for that emergency fund.

"All right. I'll borrow your car. But only because your sweet-talking ways are so convincing.''

"I know. I've been told I have that gift. For sweet-talking.''

Phoebe resisted the urge to roll her eyes in imitation of Bird. "And some people will believe anything."

"Tsk tsk, sweetpea. You're getting testy again." His grin taunted her, almost as if he knew exactly what was going on in her mind.

"Not me. I was merely reminding you that compliments are only as good as their source." She tucked the keys into her pocket. "I know you're trying to make me feel better about using your car."

"Of course I am, Phoebe. Whenever I want to smooth talk a woman and make her feel like a million bucks, I always call her pigheaded, stubborn and—what did I leave out?"

"Ornery," she said through clenched teeth.

"Oh, yeah. Ornery. How could I forget that one?" He smiled down at her and the crinkles at the corners of his eyes folded together, lifting the lean crevasses of his face and transforming them. "But be reasonable. You know you're as stubborn as a mule, Phoebe. It's part of your character. Your charm."

"My charm, is it, Murphy?"

"Umm." Anchoring his thumbs at the waistband of his jeans, he shifted, and his stance tightened the well-washed denim across his butt, drawing and holding her attention. "Maybe I overstated myself."

She made herself look away from the flex of muscle and denim. "Maybe you did. I know I'm stubborn. A little hardheaded. But I'll admit only to that little bit. Otherwise, I'm the world's most agreeable female."

"Really?" Like a big old tomcat scratching his back, he rubbed his shoulders against the wall. "Well, sweetpea, you said people change. Reckon you did, huh?"

"Go on to work, Murphy. Before I take one of your shiny pots to your head."

He laughed, eased away from the wall. "So much violence in such a tiny package. But you'll use the car, won't you, Phoebe?" Reaching into his pocket, he pulled out his paint-spattered bandanna and wrapped it around his head, tying it in back with a quick, efficient motion. "Not using it won't make any real point, you know."

"I'll use the car, Murphy. It will be a big help." Saying the words was like eating peanut butter on dry bread, but she managed. "Thank you. Again."

"I'm off, then. Take care, Bird." He ruffled her hair as he passed her where she continued in earnest concentration rolling napkins into tiny balls. "Happy trails."

She looked up and waggled one hand in his direction. "Bye, my Murphy. Be good."

"Oh, I am, Bird. I am." He replied to Bird, but the twitch of his mouth was meant for Phoebe. "I'm very, very good. Aren't I, Phoebe?" As she followed him to the back door off the utility room, he added in a low voice, "If you need money—no, listen to me." His forefinger brushed her mouth, hushing her. Lingered. "There's a box under my bed with a couple of hundred dollars in it. Use it. For any reason. Hear?"

"I hear you, Murphy. Loud and clear." She'd no sooner touch that money than she would steal from the offering plate at Sunday service.

"Promise me, Phoebe. That if you need anything, you'll use that money?"

Her bottom lip felt full and heavy where Murphy had pressed it. Scarcely aware of what she did, she raised her hand to her lip, touched it. As his eyes followed her gesture, she changed direction and toyed with one of the buttons on her shirt, worked the small bit of silver in and out of its slot. "If I have to, if there's an emergency, I'll use your stash. Sure, why not?"

"Funny, but I don't believe you any more than you believed me earlier." He shook his head. "Anyway, Phoebe, you know where it is. A safety net. Just in case."

Remembering that instant of disorientation earlier when she'd had the sense she didn't know Murphy at all, she said, "Once upon a time you were the original tightrope walker, Murphy, the trapeze swinger without a net. When did you become so cautious?"

"Once upon a time I survived adolescence. That'll usually put the fear of God into a guy. Take the keys and the money, Phoebe. With my blessing." Once more he lowered his voice. "So you'll have money in case Bird needs something, okay?" All the teasing had left his lean face. "For Bird?"

"For Bird," she agreed finally. And meant it. For Bird she'd chew her pride and swallow it again. And again.

She discovered that pride had its price after all.

She'd just found hers.

"Oh, hold on a second. You'd better take a look at the car. See if you have any questions?"

"Whatever you say." She trudged after him through the utility room where piles of washed, un-ironed clothes teetered on top of a new washer and dryer.

Not sure what to expect, she waited while he keyed in the security code to the garage door.

Nothing would surprise her. His truck was well-maintained, but not new. He might be driving any kind of car now. An old heap with a hot engine. Even the spiffy red 'vette he'd restored ten years ago. A '72 classic.

"Still have the Corvette?" She stood on tiptoe to peek over his shoulder. "I wouldn't mind driving your 'vette." She grinned. "I like to drive fast, Murphy."

"I know." He punched the last number and angled his chin in her direction. "Rita told you about the Corvette project?"

"And the brunette you liked in the passenger seat." Her mother had filled her in on the details of car and woman. Right after Phoebe had galloped off with suitcases and SAT scores to the University of Wisconsin.

"She went well with the car. Black hair. Red car. Nice combination." His smirk was contagious.

"I'll bet."

She'd thought nothing would surprise her.

The gleaming, expensive European sedan did. Four doors. Plush leather interior. Very, very expensive.

But it *was* red.

She blinked.

"I can't drive this car. Murphy, I can't. I really, really can't."

"Of course you can. You really, really can. Automatic shift. Air-conditioning. Power steering. A CD player. Hell, Phoebe, it almost drives itself."

"That's what I'm afraid of," she muttered. "This car's smarter than I am." Wistfully, she stroked its sleek, deeply polished finish. "Have you even had it out of the garage since you bought it?"

"Phoebe. Listen to me. It's a car. I like it. It's not my best friend. Drive it. If a bird does its business on it, drive the damned thing through the car wash. I told you. It's fixable. Replaceable. It's just a car."

Shoot, even she could see it was more than a car. It was a dream, a fantasy. But as she thought more about the combination of color and style, she decided Murphy's car sent a decidedly mixed message. The flashiness of that cardinal red. The stability of a car rated high for safety and maintenance.

It was the car of her dreams, that was for sure.

She would adore driving Murphy's car.

Her fingers itched to close themselves around the leather steering wheel cover.

Throwing caution to the wind and consigning her pride to the devil, she beamed at him. "Murphy, I swear to heaven, if you're teasing me, I'll—"

He lifted a strand of her hair, let it sift through his fingers. "I'm not teasing you, sweetpea. Drive it. Enjoy."

"Oh, I will." She almost shivered like a puppy with excitement. She hadn't known she was so susceptible to material goods until she'd walked into Murphy's house, seen his kitchen, lusted after his car.

"Fine. Done deal then. Here, let me give you the security codes, my pager number and the number of the cell phone in the trunk."

Dazed, she trotted after him to a long work counter near the back door. The man was crazy to trust her with that car. If she had a hundred dollars, she'd bet every one of them that the car still smelled new. Oh, she loved this car.

Grabbing her elbow and speeding her up, he strode to the counter, grabbed a pencil and scribbled on a piece of paper. "Here are the numbers."

"Just in case," she mimicked, coming back to reality. She smiled, a bubble of goofy excitement rising inside her. "I'm not used to someone taking care of me, you know, Murphy. This feels very...strange."

"I'm not taking care of you." He tugged at the end of his bandanna. "Only offering—"

"A safety net?"

"Yeah, I guess." He frowned at his boots. "I mean, for God's sake, Phoebe, you're pregnant. And you look like ten miles of bad road."

"There you go again with the sweet-talking." She didn't know whether to swat him or hug him. Swat him because of the bluntness. Hug him because of everything he was doing.

No. She knew.

She punched him lightly on the arm. "But I get the idea. You're worried about me."

"Yeah." He frowned again. "Hell, Phoebe, this is a mess, isn't it?"

"Yes, Murphy, it really is," she said softly, touched beyond words. "But it will all work out. Nothing stays the same." She touched her belly. "I'll take care of this baby. I'll take care of Bird. You don't have to worry about us."

"Don't I?" Still frowning, he lifted his hand, and delicately, without touching her, traced the shape of her belly. "Then why am I? Worrying about all three of you?"

"I don't know."

A ray of sunshine poured through the window of

the side door and dusted the hairs along his arm with gold.

Not looking at her, he stretched the tip of his forefinger to her belly button and touched her. "A baby, Phoebe. So tiny. So helpless." He shook his head. "No father, no…anything."

His fingertip was a spot of heat through her shirt, burning right through to her spine. "My baby has me," she murmured. "We'll manage."

"Yeah, so you keep reminding me." Not moving his finger, he lifted his eyes to hers. "Tony was stupid. To risk all this. To be so careless. With you. With Bird. With this baby."

At his touch, sunshine surrounded her, filled her, turning her to melted butter.

Her heart stuttered, skipped a beat.

Longing, as sweet as the sound of a whippoorwill, stabbed her.

If only….

The saddest words. If only….

"You've had to be strong for a long time, haven't you, sweetpea?" A slow, lingering circle of her navel, and then he took his hand away, lifted it to shade his eyes. "Hell, what a mess," he repeated and turned away, slid into the bench seat of his truck.

With a groan, the garage door lifted to a brilliant, hot June day.

She missed his touch with a fierceness she could never have imagined. The missing had nothing to do with passion and everything to do with need, a need she couldn't even put into words.

Until that moment she hadn't allowed herself to think about how alone she truly was.

How lonely.

Until Murphy touched her.

And with his touch she glimpsed a vision of how things could have been, should have been. The expression in Murphy's eyes had reached into her and torn something loose, disoriented her.

Even with Bird in the kitchen, she'd never felt more alone in her life. When the garage door rumbled shut, she walked to the side window and looked out toward the front, toward the driveway.

In the empty driveway, dust spiraled lazily toward the sun.

Protectively, she curled her hands over her belly and listened to the far-away whine of Murphy's truck as he drove away.

Chapter Six

Returning to the kitchen, Phoebe tried to shake off the curious mix of excitement and melancholy as she prepared herself for the chores ahead. Not that it seemed fair to see the tasks as chores when accomplished in Murphy's seduction of a car.

But they were.

And a car could only do so much. It couldn't find a job for her. It couldn't solve her problems.

Leaving Bird to her self-assigned job, Phoebe went upstairs to choose an interview outfit. Beige, pearls and heels. Exactly what a ninety-five-degree day on the west coast of Florida called for. She worked thigh-high nylons up her legs, put on a second round of makeup, and dug out the beige linen skirt and jacket that she'd decided offered the best chance of comfort.

In the mirror of Murphy's bathroom, the drab, colorless woman looking back at her seemed pathetic, hopeless. Beige wasn't her color this week, not when she was exhausted, pregnant and sleep-deprived, she decided with annoyance. This woman in the mirror didn't look as if she could control a room full of high-school students.

The black cotton shirt accented the circles under her eyes in the loveliest fashion. Very gothic, she decided, but not quite the right look she wanted to project to a possible employer. "Raccoon," she hissed.

The yellow silk blouse made her look jaundiced.

Finally, in honor of the car, she settled on a thin red cotton camisole top that tucked into the skirt and brought an illusion of color to her face. She still looked washed out and drawn, but the red was good for her spirits.

"Come on, Bird," she said as she pressed in the security code to the garage. "We're going on an adventure."

"But Hansel and Gretel will be lost." Bird glanced up at her and wrinkled her nose. "I don't want to go anywhere. I want to play in the house. And swing. I want to swing, Mama. I like Murphy's house, and I don't want to leave. Not at all."

Phoebe bit her lip. Bird had bonded. With Murphy. With his house.

Being Bird, she'd inherited her own version of stubbornness—plus Phoebe's. Tricky, having a daughter so much like yourself, but she didn't want to butt heads with Bird, not now.

Too much had been happening in her four-year-old life in the past months. They'd lived in one apartment after another. Bird had changed preschools three times in two months.

Bird needed stability, calm, not chaos and arguments.

No wonder she didn't want to leave Murphy's house.

Pondering her daughter's earnest placement of napkin pellets, Phoebe's sympathies were all with her daughter. She didn't want to leave either.

But she was the grown-up. She had responsibilities. So, once more into the breach. The battle goes to—the strongest? She couldn't remember, but she knew she had a potential battle on her hands.

And she was so tired of coping, of fighting, of keeping her chin up. Naturally Bird would smell out her weakness. Kids were incredible that way. Onward, she urged herself. Don't wimp out now.

"We have to run errands, Bird. Remember? You were the one who woke me up ready to hit the road."

"Don't want to go now." On her hands and knees Bird lined up paper balls from the dishwasher to the back door. "My Murphy will be back. When he comes home, we will go. With him," Bird insisted.

"Murphy went to work, sugar plum. You heard him say that."

"I know. We will wait."

Phoebe rubbed her eyes. Maybe the new baby would escape the curse of the Chapman mulishness. Not likely. It was a strong piece of DNA. Possible, though. She could always hope. Hope was cheap.

Hunkering down on her hands and knees she scooted close to Bird. "You like Murphy, don't you, sweetie?"

"Yes." Bird tucked her chin down and continued rolling pellets.

"I think Murphy's tired of scrambled eggs."

Bird raised her head. "Murphy likes scrambled eggs."

"I do, too. But I feel sorry for him."

"Why?" Bird kept the pellet between her thumb and forefinger. "Murphy's big. He's strong."

"How do you think he grew so big, Bird?"

Bird placed the pellet carefully on the floor. "Not on scrambled eggs?"

Stubbornness and intelligence could be a lethal combination. But once in a while, you hit the jackpot. Phoebe picked up the pellet closest to her knee. "No. Murphy needs meat."

"And peas." Bird smiled at her. "Murphy will like frozen peas."

He probably would. "And milk? Yogurt, maybe?"

"But not liver." Bird stood up. "Me and Murphy do not like liver. Remember? We discussed liver."

"You did. I remember." Rising quickly, Phoebe took her daughter's hand. "I was thinking it would be appropriate for us, as Murphy's guests, to make a nice meal for him. What do you think?"

"Murphy would like that."

Quickly hustling Bird into an outfit that would pass muster in public, Phoebe came within a hairsbreadth of having Bird pick up the pellets before they left. Understanding the significance of those small white dots, though, she stayed silent even as she hoped she and Bird returned before Murphy did.

Before they'd arrived, his kitchen had been so clean and shiny.

Now, sure, it was *clean*. More or less. Depending on whose standards she used. The counters and table were wiped down and thanks to her nervous scrubbing, the sink was a marvel of shininess. But the kitchen wasn't exactly spotless. Crumbs sprinkled the floor under the stool where Bird had sat. One of

Phoebe's scarves had snaked its way under the edge of the refrigerator. Jelly fingerprints smeared one of Murphy's beautiful cabinets and dotted the smoky black front of the stove.

She would make sure she had everything back to its *House & Garden* luster before Murphy walked back into it.

It was the least she could do.

As for groceries?

She sighed, a lapse of control but understandable, she decided, under the circumstances. She pulled the door shut, checking to make sure it locked behind them. Well, this was an emergency. Of sorts. She hoped she could stretch her fifty dollars like the loaves and fishes.

"Ooooo, pretty car. I like Murphy's car."

"Of course you do, sugar plum. I do, too. Hop in."

With her tiny fanny bobbing toward the ceiling, Bird crawled into the front seat and clicked the seat belt into its slot over her whale-printed top.

Murphy's four-door red sedan drove like a dream.

After that, the day went steadily to heck in the proverbial handbasket, whatever that meant, Phoebe decided.

She went to the county superintendent's office. No teaching jobs were open at the present. Possibly in the fall. "A lot of teachers find they're pregnant, or they move, or they change their minds at the last minute. Check back at the end of the summer, dear," offered the ready-for-retirement secretary, who gave Bird a piece of chewing gum in sympathy.

In the lobby Phoebe skimmed the packet of information concerning qualifications and requirements for certification. Apparently the State of Florida had plans for her free time between now and the opening of any possible teaching job. She slid the papers back into the glossy blue folder and led Bird back to the car.

She took Bird with her for five cold interviews at day-care centers and preschools.

She struck out. But they kept her name and phone number. "Maybe later? In a month or two?" asked the nineteen-year-old answering the phone at the last preschool. "We get a lot of turnover here, ya know."

Phoebe didn't know. She didn't like the sound of a school where teachers walked through the doors like a turnstile. But if they were willing to hire her, she could be a spoke in the wheel for as long as she could stand it. And until she was qualified for a different job.

Even though the pay stunk.

She filled out the paperwork for a bank account and checked on the transfer from her Wisconsin account. The car dealer's check hadn't yet cleared. "The weekend, honey," said the bleached blond male in the pale gray suit. "Check back Monday."

Without the money from the sale of her car, she wouldn't be able to make a security deposit on an apartment she discovered as she and Bird wearily scoured the *Manatee Creek News* rental page. "Who knew?"

"Knew what, Mama?" Licking the drips from her Neopolitan ice-cream cone, Bird kicked her heels against the bench in the park across from the newspaper office.

"That apartments in Manatee Creek were so expensive." Phoebe creased the paper lengthwise.

"We don't need an apartment. We live with Murphy now.'' With a sticky hand, she patted Phoebe's knee.

Strawberry didn't blend with beige.

"Oops. I'm sorry."

"No problem, baby. It'll wash out."

It didn't. The water faucet burbled up warm water and she scrubbed her skirt futilely.

"It's a sign, Bird. Let's go—"

"Home!" Bird slid to her feet.

"One more stop."

"I know. For Murphy's food."

Fifty dollars didn't miraculously turn into a windfall.

But it bought Bird's peas, milk, flour. Staples like more eggs and sugar. Tea. A chicken. She was tempted to buy steak. The lovely, marbled sirloin called to her, cooed to her as she passed the meat counter.

She resisted.

By the time she arrived back at Murphy's, she didn't think she could put one foot in front of the other. If she'd thought she was tired yesterday, she'd been wrong, wrong, wrong. *Today* she was tired. *This* was what *tired* felt like, she concluded as she unloaded groceries and arranged them neatly in Murphy's empty cabinets. She cut up the chicken and dipped it into the marinade, covering it with a plate since she'd forgotten plastic wrap.

While she was gone, no magic fairy had vacuumed up Bird's white dots or wiped off the fingerprints. Not that she'd expected a fairy godmother to swoop down and wave a wand, putting everything right. She stepped out of her heels and went for the vacuum cleaner.

As she grimly went through the kitchen trying to restore its glossy perfection while Bird skipped behind her opening cabinet drawers, Phoebe mentally cursed every fairy tale she'd ever read.

They'd made her believe.

In fairies. In happy ever after.

She hadn't believed in happy endings for a long time. That was the price for growing up. Giving the vacuum cleaner one final push, she unplugged it.

Putting a hand to her aching back, she bent over, working out the kinks and sharp pain. Sweat beaded her forehead. Even though the fans slowly churned the humid air coming through the open windows, she felt as if she'd spent an hour in a sauna. Bird's frozen peas were beginning to sound downright appealing.

If she hurried, she could change before she finished dinner preparations.

And douse cold water all over her body.

"Murphy!" At the rumble of the garage door, Bird raced to the utility room.

"Oh, hell." Phoebe stood up, stretched the muscles in her back and leaned on the handle of the vacuum. But even under the exhaustion, her breath hitched with the leap of her pulse as she heard his low voice talking to Bird.

As he sauntered into the kitchen, she wondered how a dust-streaked, paint-spattered male could look so cool and collected. *He* should have looked like the ten miles of bad road he'd accused her of resembling. He didn't.

Nope, Murphy, grubby and grimy and sweat-beaded, looked like a calendar pin-up from one of those calendars featuring guys from manly-men occupations. Firemen, cops, construction workers. Oh,

she could imagine Murphy's picture pinned up on
some virgin's bulletin board.

Virgins? Heck, she could imagine Murphy's picture pinned up on her own wall.

"Pregnancy. Hormones," she whispered.

"What's that, sweetpea?" Wiping his face with the
bottom of his shirt, Murphy peered at her over the
edge. "You say something?" Guileless, his eyes
caught hers. Under his other arm, Bird peered at her
with the same innocent expression.

"Not a word." She thumped the cleaner emphatically against the floor. "Welcome home, Murphy.
Supper'll be ready in half an hour. Go shower."

"I like a bossy woman, Phoebe. Nice to see that
some things haven't changed." He lowered Bird to
the floor, tugged a strand of her hair and strolled toward Phoebe.

She fought the urge to flutter her hand in front of
her face. Murphy was made for jeans. Each rolling,
easy stride drew her attention to parts of Murphy
she'd be better off not noticing.

But she noticed.

And stared, her mouth going dry at the lovely sight
of Murphy in motion.

He grinned. And took one more long, muscle-
flexing step.

Unnerved, she backed up, dragging the vacuum
with her. If her pulse pounded any harder, she'd pass
out. "And it'll be all your fault."

He hoisted the cleaner from her. "What will be my
fault?" The smile at the corner of his mouth told her
he knew exactly what effect he was having on her
poor, hormone-drenched self. And that he had no pity.

She grasped the first thought that lodged in her hazy brain. "Payback, right?"

He disappeared into the utility room. The closet door for the vacuum opened, banged shut as he thrust it inside. "Don't have a clue what you mean, sweet-pea." He poked his head around the doorjamb.

"For this morning." She plunked her hands on her hips. "You're getting even with me, Murphy. I know you are."

"Golly, Phoebe, are you picking a fight with me?" Taking both of Bird's hands, he swung her up onto his shoulders.

As he lifted her daughter, his shirt rose with his movement and a stretch of bare brown skin, muscle-rippled and taut, came into Phoebe's view.

Forgetting she was still in her beige disguise, she tried to jam her hands into her pockets.

Torture.

The devil was trying to torture her.

"Giddyap, my Murphy!" Bird thumped her heels enthusiastically against Murphy's chest.

"Yes, giddyap, Murphy." Phoebe folded her arms across her breasts. She knew what was happening with her body. Murphy would, too. "Go along now, cowboy, and get ready for supper. Bird, you stay and help. You know what your job is."

"Guess what, Murphy?" Bird tipped toward his ear. Her whisper would have carried across a soccer field. "I'm cooking frozen peas. Just for you."

"For me, Bird?" Something flickered in his eyes again, but only for that second.

"Of course."

This time, though, Phoebe was prepared. She wanted to walk up to him, cup his hard face in her hand and comfort him. The impulse was so strong that her hand twitched with the need to smooth away that—she couldn't find the word for what she glimpsed in his eyes, but it struck her to the heart.

Once, when Bird was two, she'd awakened from a nightmare, sobbing wildly, and her eyes had held that same lost expression.

She hadn't been able to console Bird.

She couldn't console Murphy.

But she wanted to, more than she'd wanted to do anything in years.

Her expression must have given her away. He frowned, averted his face, and giddyapped with Bird to the stairs. "That's it for now, kiddo. I'm off to the shower."

As Phoebe watched, bemused, Bird squeezed his leg and let him drag her up two steps before she turned loose and fanny-bumped down the stairs as Murphy disappeared around the curve of the landing.

No father. No...anything, he'd said about her baby.

Bird had paid a price, too.

And so had Murphy.

She knew the story of how he came to live with her family, but she'd been too young to understand, even later, even at eighteen, the cost to that boy, a child only a year older than her Bird.

Compared to that, shoot, the price she'd paid for abandoning her pride was zip, nada. Nothing.

A child needed two parents.

She'd never thought of Murphy as that scared, lonely five-year-old until tonight.

He'd always been—just Murphy. Smarter, more exotic in his maturity than all the boys her age. Murphy.

Dangerous, exciting, teasing. Murphy.

Funny, but she'd never seen beneath his confidence down to that boy. She'd never asked him how he felt, walking into the house of strangers.

She should have.

Careless, selfish of her never to have asked him.

Maybe she could make it up to him now. She could offer payback of a different kind. Her gift to him for what he was providing her and Bird.

Thoughtfully, Phoebe put dinner together, directing Bird to the cabinet with the dishes and the drawer with the silver. She let Bird pour the opened package of frozen peas into a serving dish and put it on the back of the stove.

Murphy was quiet during dinner, but Bird's chatter filled the silence. At some point between dinner and Bird's bedtime, Phoebe found her second wind, fatigue vanishing in the quiet peacefulness of the moments around Murphy's table.

Murphy's table that he'd salvaged from the old house.

Why had he done that?

He said he didn't want marriage. Didn't want a family. But he'd brought the table here, to this house where every board and door bore the imprint of his caretaking.

Like his jazzy red car with four, sedate doors, Murphy was sending mixed signals. She pushed the thought away to take out later and examine. Away from the force of Murphy's presence when she could think more clearly.

"Hey, Bird, want to help me decorate a car tomorrow for the parade over the Fourth?"

"Fourth what?" In spite of her chatter, Bird's eyelids drooped sleepily.

"Of July. You know. Firecrackers. Parades. Yankee Doodle Dandying?"

Bird giggled. Yawned. "You're being silly, Murphy."

"No. Not me. I'm very serious, kiddo. I have this car to decorate and I could use a helping hand. Or two?"

His courteous glance at Phoebe was more revealing than anything he'd said or done since she'd come home.

No. She corrected herself. Not home. This was *Murphy's* house, a place he hadn't turned into a home. Not hers. But all afternoon, whenever she thought of returning, she'd called it *home*. She rubbed her eyes. If she didn't watch out, she'd be as bad as Bird, latching on to Murphy, not wanting to leave.

That would never do.

"I'm sorry. What did you say? I went into a zone somewhere. We've had a busy day."

"And you cooked supper. Thank you." His manner was so formal that he might have been the guest in her house, not the other way around. "That was nice, Phoebe. Coming home to—" he gestured with his fork to the pile of pots and pans, the sink filled with dishes "—this."

Seeing where he pointed, she stared at him. "You're being sarcastic, right? I mean, this is a disaster. But I'll clean up. It's the least I can do after enjoying your car all afternoon. That's quite a piece of machinery, Murphy." Pleasure lapped against her at the mere memory of its smooth handling, the creamy leather against her thighs.

"I think so, too." He placed his fork carefully on his plate. "But I'll do kitchen duty, Phoebe. While you put Bird to bed. You look like you're going to fall on your face any second."

"I'm fine," she said automatically. "And it's my mess. I made it. I'll fix it."

"We'll see. But, Phoebe, I meant what I said. It was nice walking into the kitchen and seeing you and Bird. Even though you looked like melted coffee ice cream." His grin didn't quite reach his eyes, but he made the attempt.

"I know." She shook her head. "Beige doesn't work for me anymore. But you know something, Murphy? You have to quit giving me all these compliments. My goodness, I'll get a big head."

Bird snorted.

"Yeah, my reaction, too, kiddo. How big do you think your mom's head could get?"

"Big as a pizza." Bird's yawn stretched her small mouth from ear to ear.

"Anyway, who wants to help me gussy up my car?"

"Your red one?" Phoebe was appalled. "You're going to put cans and crepe paper on that lovely thing?"

"Nope, not that car. Another one. A heap. But it's currently drivable."

"Whatcha gonna put on it, Murphy?" Bird leaned her chin into her cupped hands. "Streamers and stuff?"

"Stuff. We can put whatever we want to on it. You think about it while you're sleeping, okay? We'll glue stuff. Any kind of stuff. Okay?"

"Glue?" Phoebe sputtered. "You're going to *glue* stuff on your car?"

Winking at Bird, he said, "It's not a very good car, sweetpea. And, yes, we're going to glue like crazy. Anything. Everything. Pie tins. Sequins."

"You're crazy."

"Probably." His grin was pure enjoyment.

"Definitely." She tapped his hand with her table knife. "It sounds like fun, actually."

"Oh, it will be. Get up early, Bird, and come help me. Sweetpea, you sleep in and we'll get your creative input later."

"Right." She made a face. "Your unfamiliarity with the small set is showing. Kids don't understand that sunlight doesn't mean automatic wake up for everyone. You'll see what early means," she added darkly.

As Murphy watched, Bird's head sagged to the table. Her eyes stayed closed. Phoebe pushed her chair back.

"I'll carry her up," he said. "She doesn't have to have a bath, does she? Kids don't really grow beans on them if they don't shower every day."

"Mom loved that story." Phoebe smiled at him, her eyes as soft and dreamy as her daughter's had been in those last seconds before sleep claimed her.

"I did, too."

"It scared me." Phoebe's laugh held a hint of Bird's giggle. "I was afraid if I missed a bath, I'd wake up the next morning with bean vines growing out my ears and nose and down my arms. Ugh." She shuddered. "Mom read to us all the time, didn't she? I'd forgotten."

He hadn't. "How could you forget? Rita read everything to us. The newspaper. Cereal cartons. If it had words on it, she read them to us.''

''I forgot. Forgetting's not a crime, Murphy,'' she said, bewilderment creasing her face.

''Books. All the time, Phoebe. How could you forget something like that?''

He didn't want to feel that resentment toward Phoebe stirring in him again, but he did. It warred with the tenderness that he felt whenever he looked at her and registered the strain in her face and eyes. Whenever he thought about her raising two children alone. Tenderness and anger.

And desire.

He was too old and savvy to underestimate desire.

He understood desire's power.

When he was eighteen and she was fourteen, he hadn't. Not where Phoebe was concerned, anyway. For a year, guilt had ridden him with cruelly sharp spurs, forcing him to keep her at arm's length.

He'd teased her, pushed her away with every means he had. Even though they'd been close until then, he'd managed to turn himself into a stranger.

He'd felt like he was cutting off his arm.

He'd seen the pain in her eyes and ignored it, uneasy with the stew of emotions roiling inside him. He hadn't known how to handle them.

He sure as hell couldn't talk to Bannister Chapman about the sheet-twisting dreams involving Phoebe. And Rita? Maybe she would have understood, but he hadn't known how to ask her for help. For advice.

He'd stayed silent, chewing on his own thoughts, sorting them out, keeping his distance from Phoebe, becoming someone who lived on the edge of Phoebe's life, on the edge of the Chapmans' lives.

He hadn't realized until now how much he'd with-drawn from the circle of that warmth, turning away from it because he hadn't felt he deserved to be on the inside, warming his hands at the fire of their love.

And then Phoebe had left.

A couple of years later, Rita had written to tell him about Phoebe's marriage and, later, about Bird's birth. And Phoebe's separation from her young husband.

And every time he opened one of Rita's letters, he felt a pinch in the region of his heart.

Oh, hell, yes, he understood desire. He just hadn't expected that after all this time Phoebe could still affect him.

The anger toward her? He could handle that stick of dynamite. It was justified, after all, and, sooner or later, they would have to settle that issue.

But not until she was rested.

He would play fair.

She was pregnant, worn to the bone and vulnerable. He could wait.

It wouldn't kill him.

And then he would see if he could forgive her. He wasn't sure he'd be able to.

Lifting Bird, he shifted her into one arm and settled her over his shoulder. Her tiny snuffles ruffled his hair. Sweet, that sense of complete trust in him.

Dishes clattered into the sink. Phoebe was rinsing and stacking, putting dishes into the dishwasher. Her color was cottage-cheese white and she moved slowly, not dashing to and fro in her usual manner.

"Go on up to bed, Phoebe. I told you I'll do the dishes." He knew she would argue. He knew she would dig her heels in until she fell face-forward. "If you don't, I won't let you drive the car," he said, cunningly going for her weak spot.

"You're cruel, Murphy." She leaned against the sink. "You know I love that car. But I'll clean up. I have to."

"Phoebe, you don't have to do a single damned thing you don't want to. It's my house. I can afford someone to clean it if I want to. Hell, I can clean it myself."

"You won't leave me anything, will you?" Her voice was small, dulled.

He got it. "This is about pride, Phoebe? About wanting to carry your own weight and not let me do anything for you and your Bird, isn't it?"

She swayed, tiredness and who knew what else cutting into her determination to keep going and not to lean on him, not to take any more than she had to from him. He finally understood what had been behind her over-reaction to using his car.

He tucked Bird's head into his shoulder and spoke softly. "Do you know how selfish that is? To be so focused on your own damned sense of pride that you won't allow anyone else the pleasure of helping you?"

"Selfish?"

"Yeah. Selfish. Think about it, sweetpea. Sometimes it's all right to take. And let someone else give. It's not always more blessed to give than receive, you know. Turnabout's fair. And pride can be selfish. Because nobody likes to be on the receiving end all the time. It's demeaning."

"Is that how we made you feel, Murphy? Demeaned?" Her voice trembled. "Me? Mama? Pops? That's what we did to you when we only wanted you to be happy? When we all loved you so much, you felt demeaned?''

"No." He walked through the arch to the stairs.

She caught up with him. Grabbing his free arm, she pulled him to a stop, her lovely, tired face pulled tight with concern. "Didn't you know how much you were loved, Murphy? I used to think Mama loved you better than she did me. Didn't you know that?''

"No," he said, and felt the world of his past shift beneath him.

Her hand cupped his face, gently, tenderly, stroking his cheek and sliding to the back of his neck. "We loved you, Murphy. Don't ever think we didn't. Because on my mother's soul, we did.''

Chapter Seven

Saturday morning, Murphy pulled on a T-shirt covered with more holes than Swiss cheese, poured himself a cup of coffee so strong it could have substituted for turpentine, and turned abruptly, spilling coffee onto his shirt as Phoebe bumped into him from behind.

"What the hell?"

"Pretty shirt, stud." Phoebe's brown eyes twinkled at him. She lifted an eyebrow as she gave his outfit the once-over. "Setting a new fashion, are you?" She sort of saunter-swayed up to him and stuck her finger through one of the larger holes, twisting the cloth around her finger. "Or is this your own version of air-conditioning? I like it." She nodded with satisfaction and her hair floated in a cloud around her, enveloping him with that Phoebe-scent.

He inhaled, taking the scent of her down to his toes. "What's up, sweetpea?" He liked the tiny scratch of her fingernail against his chest. He liked even more the way she smelled, and the way she tiptoed that same finger through the thicket of his chest hair. If he didn't know better, he'd think she was doing it on purpose.

But she wouldn't.

Would she?

And if she was, *why* was she? After skittering around him like a mouse on speed, why would she change one hundred and eighty degrees overnight?

Trapping her busy hand with his, he scrutinized her face. "I see you slept well."

"Oh, yes." She smiled sweetly at him. "Like a rock. Didn't hear you get up this morning. Didn't hear Bird. Where have you put my darling daughter, incidentally?"

"Outside."

Underneath his hand, Phoebe's fingers scrabbled against him.

"With the hose. She's safe. There's nothing she can hurt herself on. I checked. She's, uh, planting a garden."

"Ah. I thought I heard water running." She slipped her hand free, hopped, skipped and jumped to another opening and investigated it, her finger sliding along the ribs on his right side. "What, exactly, is my child planting?"

"Um, stop that, sweetpea."

"Stop what?" she asked, all innocence, her eyes all soft and velvety brown. "This?" She inched her way down toward his abdomen, slipping and sliding through the hills and valleys of his ribs and muscle.

"Yeah. For starters." He worked her hand free of his shirt and stepped back, bumping into the wall as she stepped with him, like they were doing some kind of kinky two-step he'd never seen before. "What's going on, Phoebe?" Catching her hands, he held them away from him.

"Not much. I'm just feeling…frisky. Yes, that's what it is, I think. Frisky."

"Frisky? What in Sam Hill do you mean, *frisky?*" He was off balance, aroused and baffled. He'd decided to put everything on the back burner, to play fair and give her time to heal. He'd thought a nice, long period of calm would be good for all of them.

What Phoebe was doing to him wasn't calming him down at all.

The seismic shift he'd sensed the night before couldn't explain the way Phoebe was behaving.

Could it?

Hell, how on earth would he know? He'd never understood Phoebe. Why should anything be different now?

"Is this what being pregnant does to women?" He tried to edge sideways.

She matched his steps. "Darned if I know."

"Is this how you acted when you were carrying Bird?"

"Nope." She twisted suddenly, freed her hands and worked them under his shirt, brushing her thumbs up his midline and back again, following the line of hair that dipped under his waistband.

"This isn't comfortable, Phoebe."

"No? I'm real comfortable, Murphy. I'm very sorry you're not." She nudged her bare foot in between his toes.

Her toes nestled next to his.

"Don't you ever wear shoes, sweetpea?"

"Not if I can help it, I don't. I like the feel—of

things against the soles of my feet, Murphy. Don't you?'' Her knee brushed the inside of his leg.

Even through his jeans, that light touch scorched through him. Putting both hands around her waist, he lifted her to one side. But he kept his hands clasped around her narrow waist, the feel of her skin underneath her thin top too much temptation. ''Enough. Now explain to me what you think you're doing?''

''I told you already. I'm feeling frisky.'' Her smile was a slow, seductive spread of softness and warmth across her face.

He'd never seen her smile like that, and it set off every alarm bell in his body. ''Whoa, Phoebe. Hold it right there.''

''If you're sure that's what you want.'' She ran her finger down his arm to the tip of his finger where it rested under her breast.

''Hell, yes. I'm sure.'' Bracing himself against the wall, he scowled at her, buying time for the runaway beat of his heart to slow down, buying time for other parts of him to resume a more gentlemanly position. ''Let me think about this. You're coming on to me. That's not your style.''

''How do you know what my style is? The last time we spent any time together, I was eighteen years old. Heck, I didn't have a style at that age. Maybe this is exactly my style.''

She took one more step into the vee of his legs, and he figured he was a goner right that second because his brain was smoking hot and he couldn't remember why he'd wanted to stop her.

''You like this, don't you, Murphy?'' she purred.

And then he got it.

Because he really, really liked what she was doing

to him, and she knew it. She was teasing him the way he'd teased her. But the difference was that he knew how far to take the light teasing. He knew how to keep the mood light, easy.

Not Phoebe. Past first base, second, hell, she was headed all the way home.

He was tempted to turn the tables on her, to see what she would do if he upped the ante, just a little.

But that wouldn't be fair.

She wasn't as experienced as she was pretending to be.

He was sure she wasn't, he thought, as she touched her tongue lightly to his chest and smiled sleepily up at him.

"You're playing with fire, Phoebe."

"Oh, good," she murmured and folded his T-shirt up, inch by inch until she'd uncovered his abdomen. "That's my intention. I like the idea of playing—with fire."

And then she giggled, a bell-like chime of amusement. "Gotcha, didn't I? Made you nervous, right?"

"Think so?" He wanted to laugh. Her giggle was so lighthearted, so pleased with herself, so like the old Phoebe, the one who'd been his torment and his delight. "Getting even with me because I saw you in your nightie yesterday morning and had the nerve to enjoy it?"

"Aw, that would be mean." Her hair brushed against his cheek and he wanted to bend, just a little, just enough to nibble at the curve of her ear where it glowed through the curls. "Wouldn't it?"

"Maybe." He twined her fingers with his. "Because, sweetpea, you're going to hate knowing this, but I figured out what you were up to about four moves ago.''

"Oh, heck." She made a face at him, but he noticed that she didn't move away. "But turnabout's fair play, you said. Just thought I'd practice what you were preaching, Murphy."

"I see."

She giggled again, but her eyes remained soft and dreamy.

He suspected the game had turned against her because she looked like a woman who'd enjoyed every second of what she'd been doing. In fact, she looked exactly like a woman who'd been completely involved, not standing off at a distance watching everything.

And he couldn't take advantage of that vulnerability. Oh, hell, of course he could. But he wouldn't.

But, heaven help him, the temptation was damn near irresistible.

Through the open window, a shriek of delight ripped into the room.

"Well, sweetpea, duty calls. That's your daughter, who's waiting impatiently—"

"Not so impatiently, judging by the sound." Phoebe walked to the window, her nicely curved fanny swaying to some inner rhythm and holding his gaze under the slick of shiny lime green shorts. She raised the screen and leaned out. "Bird, baby, what's going on?"

"Come see, come see!" The hose splashed water into the room. "It's a cute little bird."

"Oh, Lord. I apologize for her." Phoebe ripped off a line of paper towels and mopped up the water. "You know, Murphy, by the time we leave here, you're going to be lucky if you have a house left. I swear, I'm trying to stay on top of the mess, but your house is kind of—''

''Virginal?''

''Doesn't take you a minute to regain your form, does it?'' She shook her head and wiry curls bounced in the sunlight.

''Interesting comment.'' He couldn't stop the slow grin spreading across his face. She had no idea what she'd said. ''But that would be bragging if I admitted it, wouldn't it?''

''What?'' Her forehead crumpled in bewilderment. And then she rolled her eyes, just the way Bird did. ''Oh, Murphy. That's awful.''

''Um,'' he began.

''Stop. Right there. I know where you're headed with this. And you'll only get worse.'' Her mouth curved up delightfully as she added, ''I started it. *I* get to stop it. Right?''

''Sure.'' He was amused and curious. ''But haven't we already stopped? And Bird's waiting.''

''One more second.'' Stretching up on tiptoes, Phoebe pressed the delicious curves of her mouth softly against his lips.

Silk. Warm and damp.

Oh, God. He'd thought the temptation to wrap himself around her was *almost* irresistible.

To hell with *almost*. Cancel *almost*.

He cupped the slippery fabric of her shiny shorts and prepared to drag her closer.

The tiny sound she made in the back of her throat stopped him. It was the sound of need. Of wanting. A hum of hunger that was unconscious.

Phoebe might have thought she wanted to play with

fire. She didn't have a clue what fire could do. Whatever her relationship with Tony had been, that little hum told him something had been missing from their relationship. Thinking she knew the score, Phoebe was diving headfirst into a volcano.

She didn't have a clue what was boiling inside him. What he wanted to do with her. To her.

For her.

The resentment and desire roaring in him would burn them to ashes.

The thought of those minutes before their ashes lay cooling on the floor surged along the synapses of his mind, shorting out connections and leaving him aware of nothing except the sweetness of her, her softness underneath the urgent movement of his hands, the hot pounding of his blood.

Maybe it was the small curl of her hands into his hair. Maybe it was the way she stroked his hair back from the side of his face. Or maybe it was the way she threaded her fingers through his hair and murmured to herself, lost in a world of touch.

A surge protector popped on. The lights in his brain came back on. Reason, damn it to hell, returned.

She didn't know what she was doing.

Not fair, not kind, not conscionable, to let this go one second longer.

He rested his hands on the swell of her hips and fought the need to drag her closer, to haul her up so tight against him that she wouldn't be able to slide a piece of paper between them.

He resisted.

She'd set the rules. He'd play by them.

For the moment.

Her eyes were hazy with desire and confusion. She

leaned against him, the sharp bones of her hips pressing into him. And then she smiled, some mysterious movement of light and muscle across her face that made him wonder if he'd misunderstood after all.

Maybe sweet, innocent Phoebe had known exactly what she was doing.

As she pivoted toward the door, the shiny green of her shorts a lure in the murky water of his confusion, he decided he deserved a medal for valor.

For being the good guy, the sensitive guy. For understanding her needs better than she herself did. Oh, hell, yes, he deserved a medal.

But that slick green drew him, called to the primitive male lurking underneath all his good resolutions.

He followed her out the side door and around to the spigot. "Where's the bird, Bird?" The line was so stupid he couldn't help his own silly grin.

Or maybe it was the after-effect of Phoebe's version of turnabout.

No longer slammed up closer than jelly on toast, he was able to think a hair more clearly. Something more than playing turnabout had been behind the look in her eyes, the slow stroking of her hands against him.

There had been comfort. Sympathy.

Funny, that sympathy. He stopped, the edge of a thought nudging him. Something was going on that he needed to figure out.

Bird grabbed his hand with her muddy one. "See?" She pointed to an enormous crow strutting in front of them.

Its black plumage was glossy, metallic shading to violet on the back, and it hopped back and forth over the hose, dragging a long silver cord with it.

"It's playing jump rope with me."

"Sure looks like that," Phoebe said, helping Bird swing the hose back and forth slowly. Her arms, slim flashes of creamy skin, flicked in the sunlight. From under the sweep of her eyelashes, she threw him another unsettling glance.

He cleared his throat. He could keep his head when all about him everyone else was losing theirs. Sure, he could. "I didn't know kids still played jump rope."

"They played all those games at her preschool. And I taught her the ones I know. Cheap entertainment. And a real cheap aerobics class." Deep brown eyes captured his, a glow of—

Of what, damn it?

He needed to figure out what was going on in Phoebe's complicated mind.

Because sure as God made those damned little green apples, *something* was going on.

Glaring at her, he said, "I'm ready to glue stuff on the car. Anybody still interested?"

"Me." Bird slashed the hose once more. "Bye, bird-bird." She took two running steps and launched herself into his arms.

She was as light as her name, a thin girl-child who'd found something in him that drew her to him and cracked open his heart. He hugged her to him and then swung her to his back, where, crab-like, she clung to him with her wiry arms and legs.

How could anybody walk away from a kid like this? He could understand not having kids. Hell, that made sense. But he couldn't imagine walking out on your kid. He couldn't begin to fathom what had gone on inside Tony, what the man had lacked that made him go merrily about his way, not giving his child, not giving Phoebe, a second thought.

He'd already figured out that Phoebe had been the wage-earner, even after they'd separated. He didn't understand that, either. Why had she stayed with Tony so long? Why had she allowed him to live off her after they separated?

Her pride?

He'd thought about those questions, too, off and on through the night. The need to understand was beginning to obsess him.

Phoebe's pride was formidable. Out of pride, she might do anything.

From her seat on his back, Bird called out, "Birdbird's his name, Mama. I named him." She jiggled at his back as she added, "And, Murphy, guess what? I'm going to name our baby, too. So I've been practicing naming things. I think Armadillo would be a very nice name for our baby, don't you?"

"Armadillo? Uh, I guess that's better than Airedale." What with all the weirdly inventive names parents were sticking on their kids these days, he could picture some poor kid lugging around a name like Armadillo. "I don't know, Bird. You have the cool animal name. Maybe you want to go in a different direction for this new baby? Give it a shorter name? I don't know. I'm not good at names. What do you think, Phoebe? Armadillo work for you?"

"I'd have to meet the baby first. See if he could handle a name like that." Her face contorted with her efforts to control her expression. "That would be…an awful responsibility."

"My baby's pretty sure going to be a boy." Bird's voice sounded mournful. "And that will be good."

She sounded as if she was trying to convince herself. "A boy baby will be very good for us, I think. Don't you, Murphy?" She rested her chin on his shoulder and her voice puffed against his cheek.

"I guess. Shoot, Bird, I don't know. You're asking the wrong guy, sweetheart. I've never thought much about babies, not really. I mean, they cry. They smile. And they poop. A lot, I hear. They sound like a lot of trouble to me." He bounced her up and down, wondering what had caused that sad sound.

"I'm no trouble," she asserted. "Not at all."

His mind flashed to the trail of napkin pellets, the crumbs, the energy that came at you like a wall of water. Reaching behind him, he supported her as he gave her a good, high bounce. "Nope, Bird, you're no trouble at all. I suppose that's because you're so old."

"Of course. And I'm going to be older soon. Before Christmas. And we're going to have my party in your back yard, and you can come, and bird-bird can come and we'll have ice cream."

"We'll have to talk about that, Bird," Phoebe interjected. "We'll be in our apartment by then."

"No. We live *here*. With Murphy. We don't need that apartment." Her chin dug into his shoulder. From the corner of his eye, he saw Phoebe's shoulders slump.

And then she straightened, spoke directly to Bird, but there was a message for him, too.

"I'm sure Murphy will have plans by then, Bird."

Hearing Phoebe's words, he suddenly realized how much he wanted to be at Bird's party, to celebrate her becoming five. He couldn't understand why in the world anyone would want to put himself through one of the circles of hell that he was pretty sure a kid's birthday party would be, but he did.

"I'll come to your party, Bird. That's a promise. No matter where it is, I'll come."

She patted his head. "I know you will." Then leaning close, she whispered, "And we will have it in the back yard."

"I can't promise that, Bird. But I can promise I'll come to your party, no matter where it is." Nothing would keep him away. "Now, let's get busy on the car that's going to win the Best of Parade prize. Hang on, kiddo."

At the far end of his lot, he'd built an enclosed shed to use for projects too messy for the garage. Unlocking the hinge lock, he pushed open the door. Dust swirled in the sunlight with the movement of the door.

Bird sneezed, a sting of air against the side of his neck. She leaned forward so she could see. "G.I. Joes! And seashells." She bounced. "On the car. Is that okay?" Worried, she twisted to see his face. "Because Mama told me to be very careful with your red car, Murphy. And I was."

"I know you were, Bird." He couldn't figure out why this little scrap of a girl was grabbing his heart and squeezing it. He'd never wanted kids. He didn't think he liked kids, in fact.

But Phoebe's daughter kept sneaking in under his guard. Underneath her exuberance and busy-ness, he caught a hint of something a little too solemn, a little too sad.

That something spoke to him, called to the five-year-old boy he'd tried to forget.

"I want to see!" Bird wriggled excitedly.

In the dusty sunlight in front of them seashells, buttons and plastic lizards lined up like commas sprawled across the matte black paint of an '88 station wagon.

"Good grief, Murphy. What in the world?" Phoebe walked over to the car. "What is this?"

"Mama, didn't you *hear*? It's the car that will win the parade." Bird scrambled down from Murphy's back, her sneakers plopping onto the concrete floor as she landed.

"Where did you come up with this idea?" Phoebe laughed. "It's…bizarre, Murphy, that's all I can say."

"On television. Some guy had glued buttons, millions of them, on his clothes, his furniture. His car. For some weird reason, I liked the thought of all those things stuck onto a car. It seemed like a good idea for the parade."

"I see now that you dressed for the occasion," Phoebe said dryly. "Will you be wearing this same ensemble for the parade?" She caught her finger in the hole under his arm.

"Nope. And stop that, Phoebe," he cautioned, pulling his T-shirt free. She was still up to mischief. "We'll go casual to the parade, right, Bird?"

"What's casual?"

"That means you get to wear any old thing you like, kiddo. We can decide later. Right now, though, we have to get cracking, or we'll never finish in time. This is a big car, folks, and we're going to cover every single inch of it before we're done."

"This is what you do in your spare time, Murphy?" Phoebe traced her finger over one of the seashells curving over the car trunk.

"Yeah." He was a little uncomfortable admitting it to her. The idea had interested him when he'd first seen it, but he supposed a person had to have a certain mind-set to appreciate the sublime ridiculousness of sticking *stuff* all over an old car. "But it's not all I do." He scratched his chin, curious to see how she'd react.

He wanted her to find it as loony as he did. He wanted her to like it, to see what a hoot it was. He didn't know why it seemed important to him, but it did.

With Bird trotting beside her, Phoebe circled the car. Once she stopped, and he heard a snicker, but since he couldn't see her face, he didn't know what the snicker meant. Maybe she'd seen the row of troll dolls he'd glued along the bumper.

"So? What's the verdict?"

"I *looove* your car."

"I'm so glad you approve, Miss Bird."

"Ms. Bird." She dimpled up at him. "Mama says Ms. is better for McAllister women."

"I think she's right." He swallowed the chuckle working its way up from his belly. "McAllister women are definitely Ms. women."

"Do I rate my own section of the car, or do I have to fill in wherever you tell me?" Arms akimbo, Phoebe faced him across the car. "I'm telling you up front. I demand my own canvas. So to speak. And I know what I'm going to stick on it. Do I have to…get your permission first?"

"Stick at will. And, no, you don't have to have clearance. I'm curious, though, sweetpea. What do you have in mind?"

She stuck her narrow pink tongue out at him. "None of your beeswax."

"Very mature comeback. But you understand my concern? Following this morning's earlier encounter? You can see why I'd be a bit curious, can't you? Since you seem bent on aggravation?"

"Were you...aggravated, Murphy? Earlier?" Innocence personified, she smiled at him.

"What do you think?"

"That doesn't matter," she said grandly, waving her arms. "Anyway, if I'm going to be part of this project, I insist on total artistic control. Absolute. No censorship. I'll sink or swim on my own. Unless either of you wants to help?"

"Nope. You're on your own, Phoebe." He was amused that she'd backed away from his question. Apparently she was having second thoughts about whatever she had in mind.

"What 'counter?" asked Bird, picking up on the one word he would just as soon she hadn't. "I didn't see a counter. Only you, Murphy, and my mama hugging in the kitchen."

Phoebe's gaze whipped to his. She went candy apple red. He figured he did, too. Kids. Who knew? What would Phoebe say? How would she handle this?

She ignored it.

Seconds later, Bird was on a new track, encounters and hugging forgotten.

She whacked his leg companionably with her shoulder. "I can be your counter, Murphy. I can count a lot of numbers. Ten, three, four—that's how old I am—and twenty-*e*leven," she wound up, stressing the *e*. "I know some more numbers, too, but I might have to learn some of them again."

"You'd be a good counter."

"I know," she said simply, wandering over to a box and pulling out a long turkey feather.

Phoebe disappeared. She returned with a large brown bag that she refused to open in front of them. For a while she dug inside her bag, her face pinking with each teasing comment he tossed her way. She wandered around the shed, picking up feathers, shells and bits of plastic streamers, discarding them and moving on to another stack of boxes filled with his collections from garage sales.

They worked quietly together. He thought Bird would continue her nonstop chatter, but like in the kitchen with her pellets, she concentrated on the job at hand, the tip of her tongue peeking between her lips as she worked.

He'd never imagined that he would enjoy a moment like this.

But he did.

The sunlight shone in on them, and the heavy summer breeze moved slowly, sweetly, over them, drifted around the shed and out the other end.

He thought about bringing in a radio, but changed his mind. There was something so peaceful in the shared quiet, the shared activity. Once in a while he heard Phoebe mutter a quiet "damn," but like Bird, she worked intently.

This is what life would be like, he thought, if he'd made a different choice in his life. If he'd seen marriage as a possibility for him, maybe Phoebe and Bird, or a woman and child like them, would be his, working together on some project that made no sense in the world.

As he looked up and met Phoebe's brown-eyed gaze, he went still, glue sticking to his fingers.

He didn't want someone *like* Phoebe and Bird in his life.

He wanted *them*.

Chapter Eight

The marble Murphy was gluing to the rim around the front headlight rolled from his numb fingers.

Where had that thought come from?

He liked his life exactly the way it was. He liked his quiet and freedom. He'd told Phoebe he did.

And he'd meant every word of what he'd said.

He'd lived on the edges of other people's lives growing up. Not the Chapmans' fault or anyone else's. Living on the edge was comfortable. Familiar. He liked the privacy that keep-your-distance position afforded him.

No commitment. No mess. Life was easier. No demands. No—expectations. The word stopped him cold.

Phoebe had said dogs weren't easy. Why had he thought about a cat instead of a dog?

For the first time since the idea of the Maine coon cat had started creeping into his thoughts, he wondered exactly what kind of *mess* he was avoiding.

He scowled at the topaz cat's-eye marble on the concrete. He picked it up, rolling it slowly between his fingers. *Easy?* What was the appeal of *easy?*

"I want my Barbie on the front." Bird trotted up to him. "But she's got no head, Murphy." She looked worried.

On the other side of the car, he heard Phoebe snicker again. "A lot of people have said the very same thing, baby."

"But she's pretty, and she would like being on the car."

"I'll bet she would." Murphy tapped her nose. "Don't worry about it. Beauty's all in the eye of the beholder anyway. We'll figure your Barbie has a beautiful soul, okay?"

"She does," Bird agreed. "Both of them. They don't fit into regular shoes. But they're pretty."

Phoebe raised to her knees and peered at him over the feathers ruffling in front of her twitching mouth. Then, gaining control of her face, she added, "Murphy's right, Bird. Your Barbie will look perfect on this car." Phoebe dipped out of sight with a giggle, then shot up again. "But I don't know where we packed her."

"Me neither, but I'll find her. Don't glue any more on the front, my Murphy. Mama, you stay away from the front, too."

"Of course. Besides, I'm still working on my door. The front's all yours, sugar plum."

"Good." Bird nodded, satisfied. "I will go find my Barbie and tell her she will be the star." She vanished.

Underneath the car, a streak of pale skin caught his attention as Phoebe settled back into her cross-legged position. In shadow and sun, the curve of her thigh gleamed with gold, shimmered into darkness, a miracle of skin and bone.

A work of art. Like the old Dutch paintings he'd seen at the Ringling Museum of Art in Sarasota on a school trip, the line of Phoebe's thigh entranced him, held him motionless.

"Uh, Murphy? About this headless Barbie. You might want to reconsider your offer." She moved.

Shadow and sun shifted.

He shook his head. "Barbie will be fine. Even headless."

He rolled the cat's-eye marble under the car to her.

With a flash of her hand she scooped it up. "This Barbie is also armless."

"Kind of like the Venus de Milo?" He laughed, beginning to get an idea of what Bird's doll must look like.

"Exactly. But without the draping."

"Bird's attached to this doll?"

"Her favorite—until Barbie lost her head."

"Over Ken? The man's not worthy." He picked up two more marbles, flicked them toward Phoebe. Tony hadn't been worthy of Phoebe was what he wanted to say, to tell her that she shouldn't have wasted the years, the energy and passion on him.

But he wasn't stupid.

Phoebe had already declared the subject of Tony off-limits.

Ignoring the nagging urge to lay out Tony's inadequacies, he changed the topic.

"What happened to Barbie's head?"

"You want to hear the Headless Barbie saga?"

"Sure." He was surprised to find he wanted to

know. He couldn't imagine why Bird would have destroyed her favorite doll. But, as he was coming to learn, Bird would have had a reason.

Just like her mother, who always had a reason for what she did, whether she explained it or not.

Sooner or later, he was going to find out the answer to the biggest question of all. Not why she'd run off and married Tony before she'd received her degree. Not why she'd stayed so long with a man who didn't care for her the way she deserved.

But why she'd never returned home.

"Bird had this friend, a boy, in her preschool. They played together. Thad liked G.I. Joes. Joeys, he called them. He liked to experiment with his Joes. Different heads, arms, weapons. He'd reconstruct his Joes, putting one head on a different body. Well, you have the idea."

"Bird wanted to do the same with Barbie?"

"Oh, yes."

"And parts were lost in the rearranging?"

Phoebe's laugh rolled over him, warming him with liquid sunshine. "But Barbie looked very fetching with one of Joe's muscular arms. Until Thad wanted it back."

"I can imagine."

Fascinated by the wink of light and shadow along Phoebe's skin as she kept working on the car, he stood up.

All around him the shed gleamed gold. A slow, drowsy heat crept into him.

Summertime heat, lazy and seductive.

Without thinking, without meaning to, he moved around the hood of the car.

She'd risen to her knees.

Patiently she spread glue along the edge of a sparkly bangle bracelet and stuck it to the door. She'd taken bits and pieces of jewelry and broken glass and arranged them in the pattern of a fireworks explosion, all the glittery rhinestones and glass blended into an umbrella of falling sparks, everything coming from the bottom of the door where a layer of green confetti hinted at a park.

Arms outflung, head thrown back, a child made of blue glass bits and pearl buttons held her arms up to the sky raining sparks.

Speechless, he touched the explosion of bright jewels. "This is beautiful, Phoebe. You've created something lovely with all this junk."

Her chin dipped to her chest as she glanced his way. He thought there was something shy in the quick look she gave him, a shyness that reminded him of the Phoebe he'd known all those years ago.

Industriously, she worked a brilliant bit of red glass into her pattern. "Remember the Fourth of July picnic at Rye Bridge?"

"You were fifteen."

"You'd come home on a short leave before heading back to the army."

"I remember." She'd been so young, so trusting and filled with life.

"You had an encounter of an entirely different kind with Web."

"I remember."

"According to what Web told me later, you informed him very clearly and very strongly that he'd better keep his cotton-pickin' hands to himself, and that if you saw him trying to cop a feel one more time, he was going to find it real difficult to write his name for a while.''

''That what he said?''

She paused, but didn't look up. Her hair floated with her movement as she reached down for a flat gold earring. ''Yes.'' She stuck the earring into the center of her explosion, moved it an inch off center. ''Did you threaten to beat him up?''

''I mentioned to him that he should treat you with respect. And I reminded him that you weren't sixteen. Maybe I suggested that he didn't want to cross me on the subject. I don't exactly remember.''

But he did.

Web Brandon had a reputation for crossing a lot of lines. Murphy had made sure Web knew up front that he ought to think carefully before crossing any lines with Phoebe.

''You know that was the last date I had with Web, don't you?''

''Web was smarter than I thought.'' Murphy handed her a narrow triangle of purple glass. ''Where did you find all this broken glass, Phoebe?''

''You had a glass full of it in the pantry. I noticed it yesterday when I was putting the groceries away. I thought the bits were pretty.''

''I'd forgotten about that jar. Some glass containers I'd bought at the flea market broke when I moved in. I kept them.''

''What kind of containers?'' She stood up, clasped her arms and stretched them in back of her, pulling her shoulders back.

The delicate pebbles of her breasts indented the thin cotton of her pink blouse. A line of small buttons ran from the scooped out neckline to the waistband of her shiny shorts, a path from the swoop of her neck down to the nearly flat surface of her belly.

"Perfume vials."

She looked at him with surprise. "I used to collect them."

"I know."

She blinked, looking so much like a wide-eyed owl with feathers of hair ruffling around her face that he laughed.

"What's so funny?"

"You, sweetpea."

"Hey, no fair making fun of free labor." She wrinkled her nose and shook her head. Sparkles sprayed into the air around her. Glitter and sequins drifted to the floor like shards of broken sunshine. "You should thank your lucky stars I'm helping you out here, big guy."

He lifted a strand of her hair and tucked it behind her ear. "You'd laugh, too, Phoebe. You should see yourself. You have glue on your nose and sequins in your hair. Hold still."

She bent her head while he picked out sequins and carefully brushed away glitter, letting the stuff fall to the concrete where it sparkled on the dusty floor. Her hair was springy-soft to his touch, alive with the energy that pulsed through her.

As he straightened one long curl, sequins glittered to the floor. Coiling back around his fingers, the curl trapped him, slowed his search.

He was so intent on the feel of that softness, he barely heard her question.

"Why did you buy perfume vials, Murphy? Collecting *objets de frippery* doesn't seem your style."

"They were pretty, sweetpea. I liked them."

They'd reminded him of the line of multi-colored tiny jars catching the sunlight in her bedroom, but he hadn't realized it until now. Strange, how the mind could trick a man when he wasn't even aware of what was going on in his brain.

"Oh."

He reached out to the top button of her blouse, where a wink of sweat trembled before sliding beneath the round neckline. Her hand stopped his.

"What are you doing, Murphy?" she whispered.

"Damned if I know right now, Phoebe. Damned if I know." As carefully as he'd ever done anything in his life, he closed his fingers around the luminous gleam of that top button, nudged it free.

Phoebe didn't move, even as he walked her backward. She couldn't have moved if her life had depended on it. At that moment only Bird could have broken the liquid haze lapping like a slow tide on a hot afternoon against her senses.

Nothing less.

The shed could have blown away in a high wind, and she didn't think she would have noticed.

Or cared.

Moving her backward toward the wall, he moved as if dancing to music she could almost hear, his steps slow and graceful, his wide shoulders casting a shadow across her as his finger hooked under the second button and tugged.

She felt that tug in the deepest part of her womb, and she gasped.

He stopped, but the press of the back of his knuckle moved back and forth, sideways. "Phoebe?"

She shook her head, and she didn't know if she were telling him to stop or to continue. Her head dropped back, and she sensed the second when the second button gave way.

The wall of the shed was at her back, and weak with longing, she leaned against it. Suddenly she was surrounded by Murphy, his arms braced on the wall at either side of her face, a barricade. His hands were flat against the wall, and his arms flexed as he lowered himself to her.

His knees bumped hers.

All in shadow, all she could see was Murphy's face, his gray eyes narrowed with intensity and fixed on her mouth. He dipped lower...and lower. And then he tasted her mouth, and she tasted him, a sip of something rich and rare. A taste she would know for the rest of her life.

Heat and ice and Murphy.

She shivered, and the shiver that ran through her owed as much to the ice of an arctic winter as to a Florida summer, an assault on her senses.

His mouth moved over hers with an urgency that called to her. Earlier she had teased him with her version of turnabout, wanting only to offer comfort and lightness, to ease the loneliness she'd seen in him the night before.

She'd had no idea.

What Murphy offered now, gave, asked for, had nothing to do with comfort and everything to do with an urgency and need she'd never known before.

His mouth demanded.

Hers gave, softened, yielded to the hunger that molded him to her. She discovered she had a demand of her own as she wrapped her arms around him and pulled him closer.

No, she could never have imagined the kind of

need ripping through her, a need born of yearnings long ignored, hidden. Unrecognized.

His hands skimmed over her, pulled hard at the neckline of her blouse.

Dimly she heard the ticks of her buttons against the floor, felt Murphy's callused hand cup one breast. The arm remaining braced on the wall flexed and he was tight against her, and she was shoving against his shirt, urging it up until her skin, his, touched, melded. His heart thundered against her and she could feel every beat, knew he could feel every beat of hers.

He smoothed the skin near her ribs with a slow, easy motion that counterpointed the increasing demand of his mouth, and she sagged against him, letting her arms drop to his shoulders. Like a cat, she kneaded the tight, straining muscles.

She forgot everything in those seconds except the need to give to Murphy as he gave to her. The loneliness and hunger in him called forth something from her she didn't recognize, and astonished, she understood that what she'd felt for Tony had been a ghost of the feelings that Murphy was calling forth from her.

She could have stayed like that, wrapped around him forever....

Suddenly Murphy pressed his forehead to hers, shuddered, and braced both arms against the wall once more. Gulping air, he didn't move. His shoulders shook with his effort to gain control.

"Murphy?" She cupped her hands around his wrists. "What is it?"

Then, abruptly, keeping her behind him and both of them partially shielded by the car, he turned. "Hey, Miss Bird. You find your Barbie?"

Coming into the shed from the blaze of sunlight, Bird skipped toward them, her eyes shielded by one hand. In the other, she clutched a plastic, headless figure with impossibly long legs and arched feet. "My Barbie will be beautiful on the car, Murphy."

"I'm sure she will be." His voice was husky, but he cleared his throat and moved toward Bird, giving Phoebe a moment's privacy.

She hadn't heard Bird. Murphy had.

Quickly Phoebe tied the ends of her blouse together. The buttons were gone, rolling under the car, into the corners of the shed, mocking her cheerfully with their glow.

Skipping toward them, Bird stopped. She picked up one button that had spun toward the tire. "Why are your buttons on the floor, Mama?" She held it toward them.

Red-faced and humming from head to toe, Phoebe couldn't find words.

"Don't you think these buttons could be used for your Barbie?" Murphy stooped and picked up several buttons. "For the front of the car. To make a special place for her. Show her off?"

Phoebe nodded as Bird glanced her way. "We can make a throne for her and glue these on. Make it special."

They did.

Barbie had her throne, an ice-cream carton turned upside down and partially cut away to brace her. The pearl buttons from Phoebe's blouse rimmed the arch of the throne. If Murphy pulled the end of her hastily tied knot with a sly lift of one eyebrow, Phoebe decided he was entitled.

Thanks to his quickness, they'd been spared an uncomfortable moment.

She wouldn't have known what to say to Bird if Murphy hadn't heard her coming into the shed in time.

Without a conscious plan, the three of them fell back into the rhythm they'd established earlier. There was a difference, though.

Phoebe could sense it in the air, a crackle of electricity every time Murphy came within three feet of her. The air thickened and snapped, and she could almost feel his breath on her skin. Even when he was at the other end of the shed.

Hyper-alert, her senses buzzed with Murphy. Once, when Bird and Murphy were busy, Phoebe lifted her wrist to her nose. Her skin held the scent of him. Quickly, she let her arm fall to her side and returned industriously to her task of filling in the background of the fireworks scene.

They worked on the parade car for another hour. Bird and Murphy put the finishing touches to Barbie and her throne. Finally they called it a day. Murphy pleading starvation and Bird backing him up.

"Nice sandwiches, sweetpea." Murphy put his feet up on the swing where she and Bird were stretched out.

Bird rolled up from Phoebe's lap. "Tuna fish. Because Mama said you need to keep your strength up."

Lemonade sputtered from Murphy's mouth as he doubled over. "My strength?"

"Yes, Murphy," Phoebe said repressively. "Your strength."

He choked, and Bird clumped over to him, slapping him on the back. "I thought my strength was—"

"Don't even say it." Phoebe sent him a warning look, but it was all she could do to keep her own face straight.

"Didn't say a word." He grinned at her.

"You said a bunch of words, Murphy." Bird leaned against him. "But I didn't count them."

"That's okay, kiddo. Have a seat and keep me company." Murphy lifted Bird onto his lap and leaned back, resting his head on the back of the wicker chair as he stared at Phoebe.

They'd all taken a shower to clean up from the dust and dirt of the shed. Phoebe's skin was pink and fresh, and curled up in the swing, she looked like she'd fall asleep any second.

In a few months, she would look ripe with her pregnancy. She would look womanly, her breasts full, the flare of her hips curving out in preparation for her child.

And she and Bird would be somewhere else.

What if something happened to Phoebe and nobody except Bird was around? What would Bird do? Would she know to call someone? And who could she call? What would happen to Phoebe? To the baby?

The three of them would be alone, helpless.

Anything could happen.

Would Phoebe ask him for help?

Not likely.

"Phoebe?"

"Murphy?" Drowsily, Phoebe brushed back a trickle of sweat that beaded her forehead.

Still holding Bird, he leaned toward Phoebe so suddenly that she sat up, startled, and then laughed at him, her nose crinkling. "What is it, Murphy?"

"Who's going to look after Bird? When you have your baby?"

"Oh. I don't know. I haven't thought that far ahead. Everything will work out once we're settled, and I have a job. Don't hound me about the details, all right?"

"I'm not hounding you. I'm asking what your plans are."

Fretfully she brushed at the damp strands of her hair. "I don't know yet. But I'll handle it."

"Yeah." Keeping her from leaving the swing, he caught her elbows. "I keep hearing you say that, sweetpea, but what if you can't handle something? What then? You're all alone. What would you do?" He couldn't have anticipated the stab of dread slicing through him. "Things happen, Phoebe. Bad things."

Her glance landed on Bird. "Not now, Murphy. This isn't the time." She swung her feet to the floor. Bare toenails winked in the light. "Bird, come on. We have some errands to run."

"I will stay with my Murphy." Bird leaned against his knee. "You want me to stay with you, don't you?"

"Sure." He knew Phoebe was right. He should have kept his mouth shut while Bird was around. But what did he know about kids? "Bird can stay. I don't mind. What kind of errands, Phoebe?"

"Job hunting. Yesterday was a bust."

"Why don't you wait until Monday?" Standing up, he swung Bird back and forth with one hand gripping her two. "Not likely you'll have any luck on a Saturday afternoon."

"Not likely I'll have any luck if I stay here being a lazy woman, that's for sure," she said, mimicking him. "I'm going to put in applications at some other places. That's all. Are you sure you want Bird to stay with you?"

He wanted both of them to stay right where they were.

But it was out of his control.

And what Phoebe did wasn't any of his business.

He had to stop thinking it was.

He told himself virtuously that taking care of Phoebe was the least he could do for the Chapmans. Sure, she revved his engine with every breath she took, but that cold nugget of buried anger still lodged in his chest. He just couldn't seem to remember it whenever he touched her.

No, that wasn't quite the truth.

When he touched her, anger was forgotten in that confusing sweep of other emotions.

And the real issue was that Phoebe and Bird needed him, whether they realized it or not. And whether stubborn, hardheaded, obstinate Phoebe would admit it or not, she needed him.

No matter how much resentment he still harbored toward her because of what she'd done, he *owed* it to the Chapmans to make sure that Phoebe was taken care of.

And that was exactly what she had said she didn't want.

Thoughtfully, he studied her. Well, sometimes Phoebe couldn't have exactly what she wanted. He had to figure out what would be the best thing to do.

And when he figured it out, he'd figure out how to tell her. He sure as hell wasn't going to let her take off with Bird and her unborn baby into God only knew what kind of place. Or situation.

Phoebe could think what she wanted.

But that wasn't going to happen.

Not by a long shot.

"Bird, baby, let's go change. We'll stop for ice cream after I finish." Phoebe brushed her hair back and lifted it off her neck. "I'd forgotten how Florida is in the summer. But it's nice to be out here on the porch. As long as you don't have to move fast, that is."

"Let Bird stay. We'll figure out something to do that doesn't involve sweating." He swung Bird way out over the railing as she squealed. "Or maybe we'll go find something sticky and stinky and sweaty to do." He lowered Bird to the ground. "I have a job I'd like to take a look at and make an offer on. Bird could go with me in the truck. It's a ride out to the beach and back. How about it?" He was asking both of them.

He wanted Bird to go with him.

He wanted to give Phoebe those moments of peace.

If she'd let him.

Bird didn't give her a chance to say no.

Phoebe argued, but Murphy reckoned it was mostly a token resistance because Phoebe was a softy where her Bird was concerned.

Finally, yielding to pragmatism and her daughter, Phoebe raced inside to change. He and Bird whiled away the time taking sticks and leaves and making boats that Bird planned to take to the beach and launch.

When Phoebe came back downstairs, Murphy tried not to stare at the silky long legs in heels and nylons, tried not to notice how her tidy, belted waist emphasized the swell of her breasts, tried to ignore the way her gauzy skirt and taupe blouse drifted with her movements like cobwebs.

He tried.

He failed.

"Don't give Murphy any trouble, Bird," she said as she frowned at both of them.

He could tell it wouldn't take much for Phoebe to change her mind.

"Go on, sweetpea. Bird's not going to be any trouble."

"I'll hurry back."

"No hurry. Take your time. And, Phoebe?" He slipped her purse off her arm, unzipped it, and tucked the roll of tens inside. "You weren't supposed to pay for groceries yesterday. I don't know exactly how much everything cost because I don't spend a lot of time in the grocery store. If I stuffed too much in there, it's your fault," he added as she glared at him, her face turning white.

"Damn you," she whispered. Not zipping her purse, she pivoted on her heel. She stalked out to the garage, punched in the opening code and left in a roar of dust and high dudgeon.

"Mama's mad at you, Murphy."

"Yeah, kiddo, I think she is. But she'll get over it."

"I don't know." Bird stuck one thumb in her mouth. Her free hand held one leaf boat. "She looked awful mad."

"She sure did," he agreed, thinking about the white line around Phoebe's mouth when he'd stuck the money in her purse.

Maybe he'd made a big mistake.

But she needed the money.

She'd spent hers on groceries for him.

He looked down at Bird. "It'll be all right, Bird. Don't worry. Your mama's pride is getting in the way of reality. We'll work it out."

"Maybe," Bird said doubtfully, taking his hand. "Maybe. But Mama can be very stubborn sometimes."

"Yeah, that's Phoebe, all right. She hasn't changed." Taking Bird's hand, he led her to the truck.

Chapter Nine

Phoebe couldn't believe how fast the days went.

Two weeks and she still hadn't found a job.

She and Murphy and Bird had finished the car and Murphy had registered it for the parade and paid the entry fee. Bird was in charge of costumes.

Phoebe spent her days in an increasingly futile job hunt.

She'd thought it would be so easy. She was prepared to do anything.

The trouble was, no one wanted her anything.

There weren't a lot of job opportunities for a woman with an out-of-state teaching certificate, a major in history and a baby on the way.

In a fever of activity, she kept busy putting Murphy's house in order. Driven to repay him for what he was doing for her in any way she could, she cooked, cleaned, washed clothes. She stuck flowers in vases and put them on the kitchen table at suppertime. She turned sheets into curtains and wrapped

them around metal poles she found in his shed and
cleaned up. She took more sheets and made a cover
for his bed, hand sewing elastic at the ends so that it
looked like a lightweight comforter when she made
up the bed.

Each new project left Murphy looking grimmer.

One Sunday, in a frenzy of guilt, she ironed his
ripped jeans.

"Hell, Phoebe, the guys are going to think I've
gone too upscale. A crease in my Levi's? Sheesh."
But his eyes held a sympathy that was too much for
her, and she'd turned away and rushed to lift the stock
pot off the stove.

Intending to make enough soup to last for a while,
she'd been cooking it at a low simmer all day. Murphy's sympathetic look turned distant, and he took the
pot from her, carrying it silently to the sink and pulling out the strainer and big bowl.

After that, every time she turned around, he was
glowering at her, taking pictures out of her hands and
hanging them up himself.

She knew he was angry.

He wanted to help. She understood that. No matter
what he said about not minding that she and Bird
were still at his house, she couldn't let herself believe
him.

He would do anything for her because of her folks.

And with each passing day, his anything was becoming a burden she couldn't handle. No matter what
he'd said about turnabout, and she agreed with him,
really she did, she simply found it impossible to let
him take over her life and support her and Bird.

The situation wasn't working.

He'd tucked that money into her purse and expected her to take it, to thank him for it. She understood how impossible it was for him not to give her the money. But he didn't understand how impossible it was for her to take it. Once she'd cooled off, she admitted to herself that he didn't want her cooing at him with wide-eyed, gooey thanks.

But the problem was that she couldn't do anything for *him*.

They weren't equals.

She wasn't throwing anything into the mix. All the giving was on his side, no matter what he said. Oh, she understood his need to fix, to help. Anybody who saw Murphy's kitchen would understand that part of his nature.

Murphy was a man who took care of things, no matter what he thought. His car. The truck. His house.

If he'd married, he would have been fiercely protective of his family.

She knew that, too.

He might not have made his house into a home, but he'd taken care of the structure. The basics.

That was Murphy. Take care of the basics, whether it was his house, or her and Bird.

No frills, but he'd made a house for himself that would stand through the next five hurricanes, that would last for a hundred years if someone took care of it.

It was a house made for a family, but Murphy hadn't made it into a home. She still didn't understand the contradiction, but in her need to solve her problem, the contradiction no longer mattered to her. Time was running out.

She would be showing soon. Finding a job would be even harder then. Time was running out for her and Murphy, too, especially after that electrical moment in the shed.

She tried not to think about that afternoon.

Sometimes at night, though, her body remembered the way he'd made her feel and it flushed with unexpected, unwanted heat. She didn't allow herself to dwell on those moments in the shed. She couldn't afford to.

And she tried not to be alone with Murphy.

Because her heart skittered and banged in a way that was so new, so foreign to her that she was frightened, terrified that she might throw herself into his arms and beg him to fix everything.

In the deepest part of her being, she didn't want him to fix anything for her. She'd worked too long and too hard to learn how to take care of herself and her child. She wouldn't sacrifice that for anything.

A woman couldn't hang like an ornament on a man.

But a desperate woman could be tempted to do anything.

And she was desperate.

She left applications at every department store in the county, every store she could find. College kids home for the summer and senior citizens had already beaten her to those jobs. She filled out forms in the local restaurants, ignoring the fact that waitressing wouldn't give her any health-care benefits.

It no longer mattered.

She had to find some job, any job. Once she had one, everything would fall into place.

She tried to keep Murphy's house free of the clutter that she and Bird seemed to carry with them like the very air. But just that morning she'd seen Murphy clawing his way through the nylons and underwear she'd draped over the bathroom shower rod, and she'd doubled her determination to land a job that day or—

Or what?

What else could she do that she wasn't already doing? She'd finally been able to open a bank account with the check that had cleared from the sale of her old car in Wisconsin, but she knew that money wouldn't last a month.

Standing in front of the store-front restaurant with the Kanji characters and the English sign identifying it as the House of Sushi, she pressed her hand over her stomach, inhaled, and went in.

"Apparently the House of Sushi was looking for a waitress right before I walked in," she said over dinner that night. She dipped another ladle of chicken soup into Murphy's bowl and handed him a plate of corn bread. "I have a job!"

Whirling around the table, she swooped down on Bird. "We're employed, sugar dumpling. We'll have a check coming in."

"Congratulations." The flatness in Murphy's voice stopped her.

"What is it?"

"I'm happy for you, Phoebe. When do you start?" He laid his soupspoon across his plate.

"Tomorrow. Tips are cleared every night. So you'll have to put up with us only a little longer. And then we're out of your hair."

Bird's spoon clattered to the table, but she didn't say anything.

But both of them looked at Phoebe as if she'd lost her mind.

"It's the truth. We can get our own place soon, Bird. Liu, the manager, said the tips were good." Phoebe clasped her hands in front of her. "Bird? Come on. This is a celebration."

"No. It's not." Bird climbed down from the stool and went into the living room where Phoebe had left the cardboard boxes she'd finally emptied but hadn't yet knocked down because Bird had turned them into her personal playthings. "I'm going to my castle. I am very mad at you, Mama." Taking the stick and dried leaf creation that she'd brought to the table each night, Bird walked majestically out of the room, outrage pouring from her.

Dismayed, Phoebe watched her leave, but she knew Bird too well to go running after her. Instead, she turned to Murphy. "You'll have your house back to yourself. No more underthings slapping you in the face when you try to take a shower. You'll be glad when we're gone. I know this has been difficult for you. I know we've turned your life upside down."

"Yeah, I guess you have." He shoved his chair from the table, picked up his bowl, plate and spoon and put them in the dishwasher.

At his words, an unexpected pain shot through her. "What? I thought you'd be pleased."

"Did you?" Leaning against the sink, he faced her and crossed his arms. "I'm happy you got what you want, Phoebe. You did, didn't you?" His face was shuttered, but some tension simmered in him that made her uneasy.

"Well, it's not the greatest job in the world. The hours are terrible, and I'll be on my feet the whole time."

"Hard work," he said. His face was sculpted granite, his mouth tight.

"It's not forever. But it'll make it possible for me to start taking those classes for my certification. I can be qualified for a teaching job as soon as one opens."

"What about Bird? Who's going to look after her?" If possible, his expression was even grimmer.

She hesitated. This was the part she dreaded. "I made arrangements to fill in on my off days at the Wee Ones Day Care. They'll swap that time for what it would have cost me to send her there. And at night, she can come with me to the restaurant. There's a place where she can sleep."

"Nice plan. You'll be busy. When do you plan to sleep? Or eat? Oh, that's right. You'll be eating at the restaurant. And how do you plan to get from the restaurant to wherever you're going to hang your clothes?"

"Stop it." She smacked her hand against the table. "This is how life is for single parents, Murphy. We make do. We work two jobs when we have to, and we don't get much sleep. I'm sorry my plans don't meet your approval."

She wanted to weep.

Instead, she threw back her head and stomped over to the sink in front of him. Poking him in the shoulder, she said, "I appreciate everything you've done. If I could repay you, I would. But Bird and I have to get on with our lives, and you have to get on with yours. That's all there is to it. And we'll take the bus. Like everyone else who can't afford a car. That's life, too."

"So I see." Grasping her finger, he held it still to keep that small weapon from jabbing a hole right through his chest. "You're going to insist on this plan, Phoebe?"

"Yes." She nodded. "It's how it has to be."

"Fine. Do what you want." He flung her hand away. "You always do, whether it's the best decision or not."

"What are you talking about?" White-faced with anger, she followed him as he walked out the back door. Grabbing his shirt, she pulled him to a stop. "Ever since I came home, Murphy, you've dropped these hints. I want to know what you're talking about. To the best of my knowledge, I haven't done anything to you. What's the problem? Why do I keep feeling this nasty little rip of anger coming my way? Because I'm telling you, I don't think I deserve it."

"No?" He whirled around and captured her flailing hands. "Well, here's the deal, sweetpea. What do you think life was like for your parents after you hauled fanny out of Manatee Creek and never came back? Didn't that hurt them? Did you think those letters and phone calls would make up for your absence? Do you have any idea of how much they missed you and wanted to see you? And Bird? Did you have to be so selfish? So determined on living your own life that you couldn't take the time to drop in every now and then and let them see you both?"

"You don't know what you're talking about." Cold fury settled sickly in her. "I saw them. You know I wouldn't avoid the folks. I don't understand what this is about. I even sent you your half of the check from the sale of the house after they died. And you sent it back to me. In torn up bits."

"And you returned it to me with a roll of tape. Did

you think I wanted money? After all they'd already given me? What kind of insult was that?"

"It wasn't an insult. It was your fair share. Where are these accusations coming from, Murphy? What are you holding against me from our past? Because I'm tired of guessing why you go from hot to cold with no reasons that I can see. I want to know."

Looking at her furious, outraged expression, he found it hard to dredge up the bill of indictment that he'd kept to himself all these years. "You've always done what you wanted, Phoebe, with no thought to how it affects other people. How do you think your folks felt when you waltzed off to college half a country away and didn't bother to come home on vacations? How do you think they felt when you quit college a couple of credits short because you decided it wasn't important anymore?"

"I see. You've kept this anger on the back burner all these years? Why didn't you ask Mama and Pops how often they saw me? Did you ever do that? No? I didn't think so. You know what they would have told you, Murphy?"

Something wasn't right. Like handing her the money the other day, he'd made another mistake. He folded his arms. "What would they have told me?"

Her voice was low and cold, all its sweetness iced over with an anger that went beyond his comprehension. "They would have told you that I came to see them all the time. And they came to visit me. I just never came home at the same time you did. I never, ever abandoned them, Murphy. And that's what this is all about, isn't it? You've been angry with me all these years because of something I never did. Where was your trust in me? How could you think I would walk away and turn my back on my family?'' She took a step closer to him and grabbed his shirt. ''But that's *not* what this is about, is it?''

''Of course it is.'' His heart slammed against his ribs. What had he done?

''No,'' she murmured, her voice still blank and cold. ''It's not about me. It's about you. Because you couldn't accept that we loved you, *you* pulled away. *You* put up walls. And then when I left, what was that, Murphy? A reminder that you'd been abandoned when you were too young to understand what had happened to you? Too young to know it wasn't your fault, that it didn't have anything to do with you? Is that the source of all this stored-up anger? Because you're not being fair. Not to me,'' hands wadded into his shirt, she yanked him closer, ''and not to yourself. That boy didn't deserve what happened to him. It wasn't his fault.''

''I know that,'' he said through gritted teeth. Pain bored into him, unrelenting and so sharp he thought he couldn't stand it. He found he had to, though.

''That child was as blameless as my Bird,'' Phoebe said in a soft, tired voice, and he could hear the anger ebbing away. ''Ah, Murphy, all these years, what a waste. You've kept everything locked away because you were afraid of risking anything. That's why you haven't wanted to get married. That's why you've left this beautiful house as a house, instead of turning it into a home.''

''Two-bit psychoanalysis, sweetpea?'' He was as cold as death inside. ''How helpful of you.''

''Call it what you will. It's the truth. You've been angry with me because you thought I walked out on the folks. But it wasn't me you were angry with, not really. I see that now. You kept yourself behind all those safe walls of your easygoing, don't-give-a-damn façade, didn't you? And all the time, you were scared to death you'd lose everything if you took a risk. So you played it safe all these years. Because you didn't want to give anyone the chance to walk away from you ever again."

He wanted to argue with her, to shout at her, to tell her how wrong she was. He couldn't. He turned his back and walked off into the dark, away from his house, away from Bird.

Away from Phoebe.

He started walking down the driveway and kept on, even when he came to the road leading to town. He followed it all the way into town, past dark houses, past the local roadhouse still bright with activity. He kept walking down one dark street after another for hours, feeling mortally wounded.

Was Phoebe right?

Shortly before dawn, a light, warm rain sifted down from the heavens, drenching him. Clouds scudded overhead in a gray-black morning where only a tinge of pink promised dawn. The rain fell in silver sheets, gentle in the dark.

In front of him as he turned a corner, a deserted building loomed in the gray light. He stopped in the middle of the street, staring.

Slowly he walked toward the wooden building where boards hung crookedly and the steps had fallen off its porch.

Rusting gas pumps still stood sentinel in front.

Without realizing it, he'd walked all night and found himself where he'd begun. He'd returned to the

gas station where Rita and Bannister Chapman had
found him.

The building was smaller than he remembered. It
had seemed so huge twenty-seven years ago. Odd that
he'd never come past it in all these years. Never
thought about doing so.

Gripping one of the rotting timbers that still supported the roof, he hauled himself onto the porch and
went inside, shoving the crumbling door open.

Rain spattered through the holes in the roof. Wet
floorboards creaked and sagged underfoot. Scurrying
tiny feet hurried into darker corners as he walked
through the building.

So small.

Empty of everything except a memory.

She'd halted at the door, half-turned and waved.
She'd been wearing a white dress. He'd forgotten
that, too. A white summer dress. She'd left him there
with a soda and walked down the steps.

Murphy walked back to the door, looked out at the
drizzling rain and puddles. She'd laughed. He'd heard
her light, high laugh, the sound of a car.

And then nothing until the Chapmans arrived and
took him—

Home.

They'd taken him home.

He didn't know how long he stayed in the crumbling doorway looking out at the street, thinking
about that day. Thinking about everything Phoebe had
said to him.

The purr of an expensive engine brought him back
to the present.

Slowly, avoiding the puddles, a red sedan rolled up
the street. Rain sheeted around him, around the car,

but he could see the small face peering anxiously out the side window.

When the car slid to a careful stop near the gas station, the window on the driver's side rolled down. "Murphy, come home."

"All right." He walked out the building and to the car, feeling as if he'd been ill for a long, long time. He climbed into the front, next to Bird.

She handed him a towel from a stack beside her. "Poor Murphy," she crooned. "All wet."

"Give Murphy the rest of the towels, Bird," Phoebe said gently.

"How did you know where to find me?" Dumbly, he stared at her tired, pale face.

"I didn't go to sleep. I set the alarm, waiting for you to catch your death of pneumonia out in the pouring rain." Her smile was as careful and cautious as her driving. "I waited for a couple of hours, and then I started driving around looking for you. Finally I remembered where this place was." She looked over at him, catching his eyes. "I took a gamble that you'd turn up here. I'm sorry for what I said earlier, Murphy. I hurt you."

"We both said some hard things. We'll survive. I reckon it was time we cleared the air. And I owe you an apology. I thought you'd been callous toward your folks and I couldn't forgive you for your treatment of them. I never asked. Maybe I liked keeping that anger locked up inside me. I don't know," he said, looking out at the rain. "I was wrong."

For the next week, Phoebe maintained a cordial distance around Murphy. Her heart had broken when she'd seen his large, solid figure on the porch of the gas station. All that strength diminished by memories and loss, a loss that he'd hidden from all of them over the years.

She noticed that Murphy, too, was extra careful with her. Their politeness would have done an etiquette maven proud. Passing each other carefully, they avoided glances, bumps, even the most casual touch. It was as if, knowing how dangerous unguarded touches or looks might be, they'd made an unspoken contract to avoid them.

But something had changed between them, and she couldn't put a name to it. She'd been able to find him in spite of everything. She'd been there when he needed her.

Or someone.

But she was the one who'd shown up. She was the one who'd found him and taken him home.

That knowledge made it easier for her to reluctantly accept his offer to shepherd Bird with him while Phoebe worked.

Especially since each day made it clear to Phoebe that she couldn't work out the details of waitressing and classes and dragging Bird around from pillar to post. Bird was becoming increasingly quiet and withdrawn.

It was almost midnight when Phoebe came in from work one night, carrying Bird in her arms. She had over a hundred dollars in tips in her pocket, but she was so tired she'd almost run off the road twice, her eyes closing when she didn't even know she was falling asleep.

Murphy was waiting for her on the front porch. Silently he took Bird from her arms and carried her upstairs. When he returned, he motioned for Phoebe to follow him into the kitchen. He handed her a glass of cold milk and a vitamin pill.

"Where did these come from?" She swallowed the pill with the milk.

"I called a friend of mine. A nurse in an ob-gyn's office. She told me what vitamins you should be taking. I knew you didn't have any. Don't fight me on this, please, Phoebe. Your baby needs the best start it can have." He looked at her intently. "Speaking of which, I want you to make a doctor's appointment. No arguments about how much it'll cost."

"I'm not going to fight you. I don't have enough energy to argue about anything at this point. Believe me." She sank into a chair, kicked off her shoes and groaned.

He pulled one of the kitchen chairs close, sat down and pulled her feet up, resting them on his knees. He lifted one and began working his thumbs down the arch, massaging and pressing where every bone ached.

"Ah," she moaned. "Oh, Murphy. You have no idea how good that feels. I'll give you fifty years to stop." She rested her head back on the chair support, surrendering to the pleasure of his strong hands working out the kinks and aches.

"You can't keep up this pace, Phoebe." Low and quiet, his voice broke the silence. "It's not good for you. It's not good for Bird. And it can't be good for little what's-it, can it?"

"No," she admitted. "It can't." The admission hurt, but not as much as it would have three weeks ago.

"Let Bird come with me during the day. That way you don't have to work at the day-care center. She can help me strip wallpaper and paint. She won't be underfoot, I promise you. And I'll enjoy her company. I wouldn't do this if I didn't want to. That's the truth.''

"All right." She sighed and sat up. "Thank you, Murphy. I thought I could do it without any help. I can't. Bird's paying the price for my pride this time."

"Pick her up tomorrow after your class. You won't have to spend the morning working at the day-care center. Sleep in. I'll leave the address of the job site for you."

"Right," she said, leaning her head back. And that was the last thing she knew.

She woke up in Murphy's bed, but he and Bird had gone. He'd left the address for her on the kitchen table.

Setting the alarm again, she rolled over and went back to sleep, her exhaustion carrying her off before her hand fell away from the wind-up clock.

When she woke up again to the shrill buzzing, she laughed. Trust Murphy to use an old-fashioned wind-up, in case the electricity failed.

At the end of the day, she drove toward the job site Murphy had indicated. She found herself whistling, a light, happy tune.

Murphy took the paintbrush from Bird. "Try it this way, kiddo, with the edge of the brush pointed this way."

"Okay. I am good at this." She spread a wide line of robin's-egg blue along the middle of a wall. "See?"

"Yeah. You're doing swell, kiddo. Real swell." He smiled at her, a weird kind of pride filling him as he watched her tongue poke out between her teeth. Bird was concentrating.

And working hard.

He'd been amazed at how hard the kid worked. Like a puppy, she followed him around the house they were working on, and he'd finally realized that she needed her own job to do. He'd given her this area to paint, and damned if she wasn't doing okay.

"Is the parade soon?"

"Next week. You figured out what we're going to wear?"

"It's a secret." Slowly and carefully, she spread another horizontal stripe that overlapped the first one. "But you will like it. I think."

"Give me a clue." Popping off the lid of the can, Murphy dabbed blue paint on her nose with his finger. "I like clues."

"Okay." She stopped. Paint from her brush dripped onto her shoes, onto the drop cloth. "Me and you and Mama are going to be the same thing."

"Hey, no fair. That's not a clue." He took her paintbrush and drew a blue line down the middle of the old shirt he'd given her for painting. "Give me a better one."

"That's the clue, silly." She giggled and held up her shirt.

"We're going as—"

"As painter men!"

"I see." He was unbearably touched. "C'mere, you."

She giggled, but came toward him.

"You need a helicopter ride."

"I do."

Lifting her high over his head, he whirled her

around until they were both dizzy. Falling into a heap, he rolled onto his side and propped his head up with one hand as she began to talk.

"I know I'm not a painter *man*. I wish I was, Murphy."

"Why's that, kiddo?" He frowned. He didn't like the pain in her voice. It echoed that earlier sadness when she'd talked about the new baby.

"My daddy would have loved me if I was a boy. That's why he left us, you know. 'Cause I was just a little girl-baby."

"That's not true, Bird." He sat up and lifted her onto his knee. "You know it's not. Anyway, you're a perfect little girl. And you can paint. Not every girl knows how to do that. And you can make the best damned parade car I ever saw."

He'd never felt so helpless in his life. In the face of her pain, there was nothing he could do to erase it. He didn't know enough about kids to find the right words, to say the right thing. Phoebe's kid had this load of pain and he couldn't do a damned thing to fix it.

If he'd had Tony McAllister within thumping range, he would have done to him what he'd threatened to do so many years ago to Web Brandon.

"You're a great little girl, Bird," he said again.

She patted his hand and gave him a woefully consoling smile. "But I'm only a girl. And you don't got no babies, so you don't know about stuff like this. About why daddies leave their babies. It would have been better if I was a boy-baby. If my mama has a boy-baby this time, everything will be better. My daddy won't come back ever again, because Mama said he's busy with God, but maybe you would like us if we have a boy-baby. Even you would like boy-babies better, wouldn't you, Murphy? And then we could all be together.''

He couldn't stand the expression on her face. He couldn't stand the idea that this innocent girl-child was carrying such a weight on her tiny shoulders and that he couldn't take it from her.

Winding a strand of her fine straight hair around one finger, he stayed silent, words failing him. Finally, tipping her head to him, he studied her earnest, accepting face.

Bird shouldn't have to accept what she believed.

That was a cruelty that she'd live with all her life if he couldn't find the right words.

"You know what, Frances Bird? I don't know if I like boy-babies or girl-babies. You're right that I don't know anything about kids or babies."

Her eyes filled her small, thin face, unbearably moving as she drank in his words.

"But I know one thing for sure. I'm crazy about you, kid. A lot." He lifted her to his shoulders. "Now c'mon. You're such a great painter that I'm going to let you have a crack at this ceiling."

She hooked her hands under his chin and laid her soft cheek against his end-of-the-day bristly one. "I love you, my Murphy."

"I love you, too, kid. I really do."

As he turned, he looked up and saw Phoebe standing in the archway. Soft-eyed, she stared at him and Bird.

"Well," he muttered, chagrined that Phoebe had overheard his awkward attempts at comfort, "how was your class?"

"Murphy, Murphy," she murmured. "You're something else, you are."

The drop cloth crackled as she walked to him.

His heart skipped a beat, roared back.

And suddenly, in that room smelling of paint and turpentine and newness, a new possibility opened to him.

He smiled at her. "Let's go on a picnic, Phoebe."

Chapter Ten

As Phoebe stared at him, he strode over to her, a faint glimmer of a smile lifting his lips, his beautiful mouth curving in amusement and something else that stole her breath right out of her lungs. "Let's go on a picnic down by the river, you, me, Frances Bird and squirt here soon." Touching her belly gently, he tilted his head and watched her, his shuttered gaze revealing nothing. "And we'll talk about those plans you mentioned."

"Which plans?" she whispered, not having the slightest idea what he meant, her brain going mushy and worthless as he continued to stare at her.

"Those plans you laid out. About leaving. We'll talk about those on the picnic. Figure out what's best for you and Frances Bird." He reached up to Bird and swung her down. "You'd like a picnic, wouldn't you?"

"I have to work," Phoebe said.

"Switch schedules."

"Switch schedules?" she repeated idiotically.

"See how good I'm being, sweetpea? I'm making a subtle suggestion instead of ordering you around. I may be a neanderthal, but I'm improving. Take a day. We'll work out the details later. But come with me on a picnic. It's important."

"All right," she said slowly, not believing what she was doing. What if Liu fired her? What then? She'd used her car money to enroll in class. What would she do if she lost her waitressing job?

You'll find another job. You can cope. You did before. You can cope again. With anything. Go with Murphy. You and the baby and your Bird. Do it, Phoebe. Once more the words were so clear in her head she could imagine she'd heard them spoken aloud.

But she knew she hadn't.

She believed some other Phoebe spoke to her, a Phoebe lying deep below her consciousness, a Phoebe who understood more, saw more, than her conscious self did.

"A picnic." She shook her head, trying to wrap her mind around everything that was happening. Something had shifted and she had to come to terms with it. "I'll call one of the other waitstaff and see if someone will switch. I can't believe I'm agreeing to this, though," she muttered, heading for the door. "See you at—" she started to say *home* and stopped herself in time. "Back at your house." Why couldn't she stop thinking of Murphy's house as home? She stuck her hands in the pockets of the cotton slacks she'd worn to class and took Bird's paint-covered hand. "We'll see you, then."

"In a couple of hours. Scotty and I have to complete the primer coat on one more room before we stop. Drive carefully. But you do, don't you? You're a good driver, Phoebe. I hadn't realized how good until the other day.'' His hand brushed against her forehead so lightly that she thought she'd imagined that, too. "You McAllister women do a lot of things well. See the paint job Bird did?'' He pointed to the smear of pale blue midway across the wall. "I may have to start paying her.''

"Okay.'' Bird swung Phoebe's hand. "And then I could help Mama with her 'spenses. And she wouldn't have to work all night.''

"There's an idea,'' Murphy said gently, the ends of his hair swinging out from under his bandanna as he stooped next to Bird. "We'll talk about that, too.''

Driving back to Murphy's house, Phoebe struggled to figure out what had happened. Something had changed in her when she'd seen the loneliness hiding behind Murphy's nonchalant, uninvolved attitude. And then again, when they'd fought so angrily.

And now today, as she'd watched him with Bird, she'd wanted to go over to him and wrap her arms around both of them, take them back with her to that house that was beginning to look like a home after all the unpacking and arranging she'd done in the last three weeks.

She felt as if her life were unfurling like a rosebud, opening up to a rich perfume that she could only sense. She smiled and let the wheel slide beneath her hands.

Tomorrow.

A picnic.

The next day they went to Rye Bridge. She figured

Murphy chose it deliberately. For the memories, for the privacy.

The river's brackish black water flowed deep and quiet past them. One long rope dangled over it. Years ago they'd hung onto the rope, leaping off the edge of the bluff and swinging as far out as they could before releasing the rope and dropping into the murky depths.

Half-asleep in the hot sunshine, lying on the blanket they'd placed on the low bank of the river, she felt a tickle down her nose, trailing over her mouth and back again. Opening her eyes, she saw Murphy looking down at her, his lean face more serious than she'd ever seen it before. His hair swung forward, half-hiding his face.

"Where's Bird?" she asked drowsily. She'd been dreaming of Murphy and Bird. And a baby whose face she couldn't see. Lights had twinkled around them, glowed. She shook her head. Silly dreams. "Where's my darling daughter?"

"Making mud pies. I can see her. She's fine. And, yes, she still has her life jacket on."

"So why did you want to come on a picnic, Murphy?" Teasing, she hooked her finger in the edge of his swimsuit and tugged him toward her, much as he had done to her weeks earlier. "Because you're up to something, aren't you?"

"Frances Bird needs a father, Phoebe. So does this one." Ever so slowly, just as he'd eased the sequins and glitter out of her hair that day in the shed, he spread his palm flat over the slight swelling of her belly. "Marry me. Let me be a father to them. A husband to you."

Her throat closed tight with longing, with regret.

"What a sacrifice, Murphy. To give up your plans for your life. To sacrifice them for us." She cupped his cheek, let her fingers smooth the lines there. "You work so hard. And you're so kind. I never knew how kind you were." She let her thumb brush against the shape of his mouth. She loved his mouth.

She loved him, she realized.

She always had.

All those terrors that had sent her racing away from Manatee Creek, all those emotions and longings she hadn't understood back then—all because she'd loved Murphy with everything in her young heart.

Loved him still.

Loved him too much to let him make that kind of sacrifice. She'd thought she could do anything for her children.

But she couldn't do this.

She couldn't accept his sacrifice.

Murphy deserved someone he could love whole-heartedly with nothing from the past shadowing that love, nothing to remind him of his past and the mother who'd walked away.

"Murphy, I can't," she murmured through lips numb with the effort of not accepting his offer. "You can't marry someone out of a misguided sense of responsibility. Out of pity." She pressed her hand over his lips and felt their cool, slick surface move against her skin. "I know. You'll argue that you're not doing it for any of those reasons. But I know you, Murphy, maybe better than you know yourself. Pity, responsibility, kindness—oh, Murphy, these are not reasons to marry someone."

With every word she said, his hand remained

lightly on her, a warm, comforting weight that seemed to go right down to the baby in her womb.

She knew it was too early, knew it wasn't possible, but as Murphy's hand moved against her, she would have sworn she felt her baby move.

Imagination again.

Nothing more, but she found her mouth opening and the words coming out, words she'd been determined not to say.

"All right. I'll marry you." The words were spoken before she realized she'd said them out loud. Openmouthed, she stared up at him, half-reaching up to snatch the words from the air.

"Too late, Phoebe," Murphy whispered, reading her mind in the intake of breath she made. He leaned so close that his hair tickled her cheek and his springy-soft chest hair brushed against her, sending urgent signals throughout her traitorous body. "You can't take the words back, sweetpea."

She wanted to.

She knew she should.

She tried to.

Murphy wouldn't let her.

No matter how hard she tried to take him aside and get him alone so that she could straighten things out, she couldn't.

He was never alone.

He and Frances Bird seemed to have made a pact to become each other's shadow. Everywhere Murphy went, Bird went trotting after, as if some invisible string connected her to him.

And Bird blossomed.

Watching Murphy's effect on her child, Phoebe felt

herself being torn apart. She loved Murphy. She loved her child.

But how could she let Murphy throw himself on the altar of some imagined obligation? Over the years, he would regret what he was trying so hard to do.

How could she even think of doing this to him?

She painted woodwork white in one of the bedrooms they'd decided would be the baby's.

She, Murphy and Bird picked out paint for the room that would be Bird's.

And Phoebe went into a panic attack with each new purchase.

She continued to work at the House of Sushi. She wasn't about to quit. She was too terrified. She didn't want to return to that woman who'd shown up on Murphy's front step with nothing except the fifty dollars in her pocket.

Never again.

She wanted to make this marriage work.

She wanted to cancel it.

Three days before the wedding, storms hovered off shore in the Gulf. The falling barometric pressure made her cranky and irritable. Her hair turned into a Medusa's nest of curls, and she felt like crying every time Bird or Murphy looked at her.

They were going to have an actual church wedding. The three of them had agreed on that, but Bird opted for a Hamburger Hoedown reception. Catered. So they could have the party in the back yard.

"Or some people could have hot dogs," she added on second thought. "'Cause some people don't like cow meat, you know. So we have to have choices. And we got to have Napoleon ice cream."

Murphy said that sounded real cool to him. He was all for choices and Napoleon ice cream, too.

The wedding would be small. Scotty and four of the men from Murphy's remodeling crew were coming with their wives. Phoebe had invited several of the people in her Behavior Modification class, but she was coming to believe that her own behavior was in dire need of modification.

They shopped for a crib, and her heart cracked as Murphy came along, throwing in his two cents' worth and teasing Bird, tossing her into one crib and saying, "Now I see what I missed. You must have been a hell of a cute baby, kid. Wish I'd been there."

Phoebe wished he'd been there, too.

Tony hadn't been. Bird hadn't had a male in her life except for Thad, the G.I. Joe destroyer, since shortly after she was born. But she had Murphy now.

And so did Phoebe.

But she couldn't rid herself of the nagging feeling that this was the absolutely, unquestionably worst decision she'd ever made in a lifetime of bad decisions.

The night before the wedding, she fled to the porch swing. She needed to get away from the constant energy of Murphy and Bird.

"You're bad influences on each other," she'd scolded them before tromping out to the swing and collapsing into it.

Lying there, she commiserated with herself. Her back hurt. Her hair looked as if she'd run her fingers through it and stretched it out like rubber bands, letting it snap back into chaotic, uncontrollable curls.

She felt as if she were flying headfirst into a bottomless canyon. Terror cramped her insides with cold claws of dread, and there was nothing she could do to call the whole avalanche off.

It just kept rolling, rolling, rolling on over her.

Lying in the swing with her feet propped up on the armrest, she gave way to a small hiccup of tears.

The screen door creaked open.

In spite of the darkness, she knew it was Murphy.

He sank down at the end of the swing and lifted her feet into his lap. "Scared, aren't you, sweetpea?"

"To death," she said mournfully. "To death. Let's not do this, Murphy. We're making a mistake."

"Too late. The hot dogs have been delivered. We're stuck. Don't you know you can't cancel a wedding once the hot dogs have arrived?"

"I never heard that," she said on a hiccup and wiped her eyes dry with the hem of her shirt.

"It's a rule," he added earnestly. "I must have read it in a bride book somewhere."

Wrapped in heat and darkness with no stars breaking the deep black-velvet night, she took her courage in hand once more. "Murphy, I can't let you take on the responsibility of me and my two babies. You never wanted a family. You never wanted this kind of life, and now you're plunging into everything you've always avoided. You can't escape kids, Murphy. Once they work their sneaky way into your heart, they're there, camped forever. And it's scary. You don't get to sleep. You don't get a vacation from thinking about them and worrying—oh, Murphy, you can't imagine how much worrying." Tears started leaking again. "And this—" she swiped at her eyes "—you have to put up with a pregnant bride maxing out on hormones and swinging from one mood to the next. This isn't what you want, Murphy, believe me.

It can't be." She hiccuped noisily, her snuffles loud and heartfelt.

"Here, sweetpea." He handed her his bandanna. "Blow."

She sobbed. Of course Murphy would have a handkerchief when she needed it the most. "You're so good," she wailed, "and I'm going to ruin your life. And we'll be a burden—"

"Shut up, Phoebe," he finally said. "Here's the deal. I want to marry you. I want to be Frances Bird's father. I'm making a choice here, you know."

She wanted him to tell her he loved her. She didn't want to hear about his willingness to bear the responsibility of her and her children. After all the lonely years, she wanted more.

She wanted the whole enchilada.

Love, babies and Murphy.

Struggling to sit up, to tell him what she wanted, she felt the brush of his hand against her face, stopping her words. "Shh, Phoebe. Don't worry so much. Take a deep breath and listen to the night."

In the dark, his slow movement finally stilled her restless actions. Once more, as he had at Rye Bridge, Murphy spread his wide, rough palm over her belly. This time, though, he leaned forward and placed his mouth gently over her belly button. Soft, dark as the night, his words seeped into her.

"Hey, Phoebe's baby. Can you hear me in there? I have some things to tell you. Things you need to know before you come bursting into this beautiful world. So listen up, hear? You have the most beautiful mother in the world, kid."

"But I'm going to be huge in another few

months," Phoebe sobbed again. "And you'll be sorry you decided to do this."

"Shut up, sweetpea. You're interrupting our conversation."

Caught between tears and giggles, she shut up.

"And you're going to have the greatest sister anybody could ever hope for. But she's going to give you a run for your money, kid, so come out prepared."

Half-sitting now, Phoebe threaded her hands through Murphy's hair. "You fool."

"I'm not finished." He looked up from her belly. "So hold your horses a little longer." Putting his mouth on her belly button once more, he spoke again, his breath dampening the cotton of her shirt as he made a pledge. "I'm going to marry your mother because I love her, and I love Frances Bird. But I take thee, too, Phoebe's baby, to be my lawfully wedded child. To have and to hold. To be mine in sickness and in health. To raise. To cherish. To love. Now and forever." His lips were warm against her bare belly as he finished.

The words captured her, held her in a web of love the likes of which she'd never known. "You really love me, Murphy?"

He nodded. "Of course I do. I've loved you since the first day I saw you. You were going to be my sister, and I loved you then. And then I fell in love with you when I was seventeen. But it scared me. Because I was so confused I didn't know left from right. It took me a while to grow up enough to love you right, Phoebe, but I do with all my heart. With all my soul."

She reached up to cup his dear, dear face, the face she'd loved all her life.

And then he asked her a question she would never have expected, but she could hear that it came from a place inside him that had never seen the light of day. "Phoebe, you can trace your ancestry back to the revolution and before. But I don't know who I am, where I come from."

Such pain in his husky voice that she ached for him, but he continued, not letting her speak.

"Will that be good enough for your babies? For you? Because I sure can't see how it will be." He let his hand drift over her belly, soothing, stroking, and she wanted to weep for him, for the years of loneliness and emptiness that he'd endured, for the pain she now understood and wanted to take from him.

Before he could say anything else, she stopped him. "I love you, Murphy Jones, no matter who you are or where you came from. That doesn't matter. You're mine now." Placing his free hand over her heart, she whispered, returning his pledge with one of her own, "This is your place, Murphy. Forever."

In the silence before he answered her, she heard the thunder of his heart against hers, or maybe it was only the distant rumble of summer lightning bringing the storms that had been threatening. She sensed the breath he took, a breath so deep that it was almost as if he were throwing off chains. Gathering her close to him, he took one more shuddering breath. His voice rough with emotion, he asked, "Is it tomorrow already? Because I'm marrying you, Phoebe, you and your babies, come hell or high water."

"Midnight. Close enough," she giggled, understanding what he wanted. "Will that do?"

Touching his mouth, she traced its shape in the

darkness, grateful for the twists and turns of fate that had brought her home again.

Home to this house. Home to Murphy.

Burying his face in her hair, he whispered teasingly, his voice curling deep inside her, down to her womb, "So I reckon you mean a college girl can love a blue-collar man, huh?"

Slyly, letting her teeth nip at his ear, she replied, "I don't know about a college girl, but a college woman? Oh, believe it, Murphy, believe it. Because I do." She answered his deepening kiss with one of her own, her heart and soul in the touch of her hand along his jaw, against his heart.

And so they were wed, with confetti, hot dogs, hamburgers and grape juice. Wed with the love of their friends who gathered in the back yard on a day so hot and humid that the bride went barefooted and wore a gauzy cotton dress of pale peach.

The groom, waiting for her in his best linen slacks and jacket, grabbed her hand the second he could. The two people seated nearest them in the semicircle on the grass swore the groom asked the bride if she ever intended to wear another pair of shoes.

The thin child walking up the grass path toward them took both their hands, and, in a clear, piping voice, said, "I give you both away to each other. And to me, too, because my Murphy will always be mine."

One of the same two people seated on the grass later insisted that the groom's gray eyes had grown shiny with unshed tears, but that the bride, oh, the bride's tears slipped down her smooth cheeks like dew down a rose petal.

But he was Irish and given to whimsy.

And on the Fourth of July when the Joneses, all three and a half of them, laughed their way up the pedestal stairs to accept the trophy for the best parade car, no one would have disagreed with those who said that they were so crazy in love that the air hummed around them.

A cynic might have, but then cynics seldom go to Fourth of July parades and cheer for cars with feathers and buttons and headless Barbies enthroned in busted-off pearl buttons.

Epilogue

Shiny gold ribbon spiraled off the edge of Murphy's double bed. Sheets of red and green wrapping paper lay in billowing rivers on the floor. Watery winter sunlight shimmered through the window, glimmered against the richness of paper and ribbons. One wrinkled sheet of candy cane printed paper floated up from the floor as a huge orange and white Maine coon cat wriggled free and leaped to the bed, shaking it.

"Hey, fat boy! Easy there." Murphy reached a protective arm toward Phoebe and the baby as the cat and Bird both gave one more bounce. The bedsheet slipped down to his waist as he leaned forward and tickled the purring cat's chin.

Phoebe felt like purring herself as she watched Murphy's big, strong hand stroking the cat.

Accepting Murphy's homage, King Tut gave a final chirp, padded back to the end of the bed and kneaded the comforter, finally settling into a tight, very large ball. Both of his marmalade eyes stared without winking at Murphy, Phoebe, Bird and baby.

Looking at Phoebe over his bare shoulder, Murphy grinned wickedly. "I love my Christmas present, sweetpea."

"And which one would you be talking about?" Shifting baby Bannister Murphy Jones to her left arm, she tapped the warm, smooth skin of his arm, feeling the ripple of his response under her light touch. "Probably the shaving lotion?" She made her eyes wide and innocent.

"That, too." His grin widening, he shifted, sliding closer to her. "I like *all* of my presents, sweetheart." He let his leg slide against hers under the weight of the covers. His hip nudged a tiny bit closer.

"Do you now?" Settling Ban against her breast, she leaned against Murphy's shoulder.

He slid down the headboard, making it easier for her to rest against him. "Oh, maybe some a tad more than others." He ran one long finger down her throat, down the slope of her breast, letting his hand linger before resting it against Ban's cheek.

Ban gurgled happily. Waving one tiny fist wildly, he flailed at Murphy's hand. Finally catching one finger in his tiny fist, he held on for dear life.

Phoebe saw the blurred gray of Murphy's eyes before he turned to her daughter, who was rocking back and forth at the end of the bed.

"C'mere, Bird." His voice husky, Murphy caught the edge of Bird's nightgown with his free hand, plopping her into the nest of his sheet and comforter-draped lap.

She handed him a candy-striped ribbon. "So I can be festive, my Murphy." Facing him, she scrunched her face and studied him. "Okay?" A slight frown creased her thin face. "You can tie me a bow?"

"For you, kiddo?"

As Phoebe watched, her heart brimming with a happiness so strong that it came close to terrifying her, Murphy rubbed his nose against Bird's.

"For you, Bird, anything." He took the ribbon and slowly, never taking his eyes from Bird's face, he solemnly wove the ribbon through Bird's flyaway hair, tying the ribbon into five loops. "For you, kiddo, I can even do hair ribbons." He frowned as the bow started to slip down Bird's fine hair. Catching it, he retied the glossy ribbon. "Yep. The moon. The stars. I'd give it all to you. Because you're my very own Bird." He gave a pat to the ribbon, his hand lingering against the small shape of her daughter's head.

Bird nodded once, cautiously. "That's what I thought. I was worried, though." Like Phoebe, she leaned against Murphy, the four of them all touching in the quiet room. But Bird's expression was still troubled.

Phoebe knew Bird didn't mean hair ribbons. Phoebe herself had worried that the new baby would upset Bird's growing confidence and happiness. Even before Ban arrived, she worried. About her mood swings. About Bird. About everything.

But Murphy? Ah, Murphy had sailed through the days of her pregnancy, laughing at her crankiness, washing her hair with long, slow strokes, massaging her back. And, most of all, oh, most of all, he'd taken Bird everywhere with him, his tenderness changing her daughter like sunlight spilling onto ready ground after a cold winter.

"I know you were worried, Frances Bird." He

placed both hands on either side of Bird's face. "But you shouldn't have been."

Not saying anything, Bird nodded again, but her expression didn't change.

Reaching around her, Murphy found the gold Christmas balloon Bird had wrapped in wads of red paper and ribbon and given him. He placed it to his mouth and blew. "See?"

Bird lifted her head, watched him carefully.

"You love your Mama as much as ever, don't you? Even though I'm here, the baby's here, you don't love your Mama any less just because you have more people to love, do you?"

"No."

"And you love King Tut, too, even though he's plunked into our lives, right?"

"Yes." Bird's puzzlement was almost palpable, and Phoebe wondered where Murphy was heading with his energetic puffing on the balloon.

"Well, kiddo, that's how love is. There's room for everybody. Like a balloon. The more love you have to give, the more room there is. You just keep adding to it and it stretches and stretches."

Phoebe sent a prayer winging heavenward that the balloon wouldn't pop.

And then, stunned, she realized that Murphy wouldn't let that happen. Murphy would take care of that, too.

"Like Mama's belly stretched with baby Ban?" Bird cocked her head.

"Sort of." Murphy cleared his throat.

Phoebe giggled.

"Okay." Patting Ban's downy head gently and carefully, Bird tipped forward and whispered loudly into his minute shell of an ear, "It's okay, Banny baby. You'll like having a sister. And don't worry," she added in consolation, patting his nose as he stared with deep brown eyes back at her, "being a boy won't be too bad 'cause you got me and Murphy to 'splain it all to you."

"Good thing, huh?" Murphy's low voice tingled down Phoebe's spine.

Swaying between them, Bird cooed at Ban, "You'll like this family, baby. You'll like us, and I love being married."

"Me too." Phoebe's voice melded with Murphy's deeper one in stereo, and Bird giggled.

Looking down at the fuzzy head of her baby and the only slightly darker hair of Bird, Phoebe felt her heart swell, felt such a wave of love sweep over her that she couldn't catch her breath.

And then she met Murphy's laughing, clear-eyed gaze and breath came back in a rush.

At the foot of their bed, his purrs reverberating noisily, King Tut closed his eyes sleepily and stretched out one huge paw, resting it against Murphy's leg. Phoebe blinked back tears of joy. In her arms, touching her, her whole world was there. Murphy. Bird. Ban.

Her own Christmas miracle.

She lifted one hand and cupped it against Murphy's cheek. Against his skin her hand was pale, and her old-fashioned wedding ring, a ring he'd discovered in an antique shop, glinted in the sunlight.

She took a deep breath, warmth curling down to her toes.

Finally, at last, she was home.

* * * * *

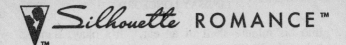

Silhouette ROMANCE™

Join *Silhouette Romance*
as more couples experience
the joy only babies
can bring!

Bundles of Joy

September 1999
THE BABY BOND
by Lilian Darcy (SR #1390)

Tom Callahan a daddy? Impossible! Yet that was before Julie Gregory showed up
with the shocking news that she carried his child. Now the father-to-be knew
marriage was the answer!

October 1999
BABY, YOU'RE MINE
by Lindsay Longford (SR #1396)

Marriage was the *last* thing on Murphy Jones's mind when he invited
beautiful—and pregnant—Phoebe McAllister to stay with him. But then
she and her newborn bundle filled his house with laughter...and had bachelor
Murphy rethinking his no-strings lifestyle....

And in December 1999, popular author

MARIE FERRARELLA

brings you

THE BABY BENEATH THE MISTLETOE (SR #1408)

Available at your favorite retail outlet.

Silhouette®

Look us up on-line at: http://www.romance.net   SRBOJS-D

If you enjoyed what you just read,
then we've got an offer you can't resist!

Take 2 bestselling love stories FREE!

Plus get a FREE surprise gift!

Clip this page and mail it to Silhouette Reader Service™

IN U.S.A.	IN CANADA
3010 Walden Ave.	P.O. Box 609
P.O. Box 1867	Fort Erie, Ontario
Buffalo, N.Y. 14240-1867	L2A 5X3

YES! Please send me 2 free Silhouette Romance® novels and my free surprise gift. Then send me 6 brand-new novels every month, which I will receive months before they're available in stores. In the U.S.A., bill me at the bargain price of $2.90 plus 25¢ delivery per book and applicable sales tax, if any*. In Canada, bill me at the bargain price of $3.25 plus 25¢ delivery per book and applicable taxes**. That's the complete price and a savings of over 10% off the cover prices—what a great deal! I understand that accepting the 2 free books and gift places me under no obligation ever to buy any books. I can always return a shipment and cancel at any time. Even if I never buy another book from Silhouette, the 2 free books and gift are mine to keep forever. So why not take us up on our invitation. You'll be glad you did!

215 SEN CNE7
315 SEN CNE9

Name	(PLEASE PRINT)	
Address	Apt.#	
City	State/Prov.	Zip/Postal Code

* Terms and prices subject to change without notice. Sales tax applicable in N.Y.
** Canadian residents will be charged applicable provincial taxes and GST.
All orders subject to approval. Offer limited to one per household.
® are registered trademarks of Harlequin Enterprises Limited.

SROM99   ©1998 Harlequin Enterprises Limited

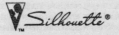

Silhouette ROMANCE™

VIRGIN BRIDES

Your favorite authors tell more heartwarming stories of lovely brides who discover love... for the first time....

July 1999 GLASS SLIPPER BRIDE
Arlene James (SR #1379)
Bodyguard Jack Keller had to protect innocent Jillian Waltham—day and night. But when his assignment became a matter of temporary marriage, would Jack's hardened heart need protection...from Jillian, his glass slipper bride?

September 1999 MARRIED TO THE SHEIK
Carol Grace (SR #1391)
Assistant Emily Claybourne secretly loved her boss, and now Sheik Ben Ali had finally asked her to marry him! But Ben was only interested in a temporary union...until Emily started showing him the joys of marriage—and love....

November 1999 THE PRINCESS AND THE COWBOY
Martha Shields (SR #1403)
When runaway Princess Josephene Francoeur needed a short-term husband, cowboy Buck Buchanan was the perfect choice. But to wed him, Josephene had to tell a *few* white lies, which worked...until "Josie Freeheart" realized she wanted to love her rugged cowboy groom forever!

Available at your favorite retail outlet.

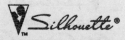